THE WOLFMAN HAD FOUL BREATH

His initial leap knocked Harry over. He snarled and snapped, trying to get at Harry's throat with his teeth. Straining, Harry brought up his knees and dealt the wolfman a heavy blow in the crotch.

The wolfman howled in pain, momentarily pre-occupied.

Harry rolled free of him, rose to his knees. He aimed his .38 revolver at the wolfman. "Back off or I'll use this."

Growling, the wolfman lunged again. His paws raked at Harry.

Harry fired.
Again.
Twice more.
Bullets failed to stop him . . .

Ron Goulart

THE PRISONER OF BLACKWOOD CASTLE

AVON
PUBLISHERS OF BARD, CAMELOT, DISCUS AND FLARE BOOKS

THE PRISONER OF BLACKWOOD CASTLE is an original publication of Avon Books. This work has never before appeared in book form. This work is a novel. Any similarity to actual persons or events is purely coincidental.

AVON BOOKS
A division of
The Hearst Corporation
·1790 Broadway
New York, New York 10019

Copyright © 1984 by Ron Goulart
Published by arrangement with the author
Library of Congress Catalog Card Number: 84-91079
ISBN: 0-380-88005-9

First Avon Printing, July, 1984

AVON TRADEMARK REG. U. S. PAT. OFF. AND IN OTHER COUNTRIES, MARCA REGISTRADA, HECHO EN U. S. A.

Printed in the U. S. A.

WFH 10 9 8 7 6 5 4 3 2 1

Chapter 1

Zevenburg in the spring of 1897 was a magnificent and glittering city. Capital of Orlandia, that small sovereign nation on the eastern fringes of the vast Habsburg Empire, Zevenburg was known worldwide as a metropolis where existence is more beautiful, joy more easily obtained and trouble more quickly thrown away than anywhere else. Its overall mood was especially festive that spring, because its splendid Quadricentennial Exposition had opened only three weeks earlier, and eager visitors were flocking to this gleaming city on the River Fluss from all over Europe and beyond. True, benevolent old King Ulrich was rumored to be slowly dying in his shadowy chambers in the ornate palace on Mariahilferstrasse. But he had had a long happy reign and would be succeeded by the popular and beautiful Princess Alicia. Business, in everywhere from the great hotels to the tiny shops, had never been better, and the weather had held pleasant and serene for nearly a full week.

And so nearly everyone in Zevenburg on the tranquil spring evening on which our story commences was content and happy, with the exception of old

King Ulrich, who was justifiably downcast about his imminent death, and Harry Challenge.

Harry had just been thrown out of the palace, thrown out by two gilded and overdressed footmen on the explicit orders, so they claimed as they tossed Harry onto the hard cobblestones of the twilit Mariahilferstrasse, of Princess Alicia herself.

"Well, damn," remarked Harry, rising up from beside a curbside border of freshly bloomed flowers and glancing around for his bowler hat.

"Your hat, swine!" called one of the burly brass-buttoned footmen as he pegged the dented headgear out through the high wrought-iron gateway of the palace grounds.

"Much obliged." Harry caught the sailing hat out of the air, poked out the most conspicuous dents and tapped it onto his head.

A closed carriage went clopping by, heading for the Ulrichplatz and trailing light feminine laughter.

Harry was a man of middle height, lean, clean-shaven and a shade weather-beaten. He was not quite a year beyond thirty, and in the course of pursuing his profession he had killed several men. In fact, beneath the coat of his dark suit he wore a Colt .38 revolver in a snug shoulder holster. It was one of his rules, however, never to shoot anyone in anger.

Besides which, the two louts who'd heaved him out into the growing dusk had apparently been acting on orders from the fair Alicia.

"Women are changeable," Harry reminded himself as he brushed the dust of Mariahilferstrasse from his clothes and started walking away from the high-walled palace grounds. "No reason for the princess to be any—"

Slowing, he glanced back over his shoulder. The

new electric lamps were late in coming on tonight, and the darkness that stretched out behind him was thick. Harry narrowed his eyes, scrutinizing one particular linden tree some hundred yards behind him.

After a few seconds, he decided there wasn't anyone watching from behind that tree after all. He lit one of the thin black cigars he favored and resumed walking.

"Things sure can change one hell of a lot in just over a year," he said to himself as he thought of the lovely golden-haired princess.

Zevenburg was noted for its profusion of sidewalk cafes, and one of the most popular, as many know, was Penzler's. Located in a twisting lane off Prinz Rollo Strasse and bordered by a row of lilac trees, it was always crowded with a mixture of discriminating local denizens and well-to-do tourists.

At a few minutes past the hour of seven on the evening in question, a portly man in a gray suit, flamboyant double-breasted waistcoat and astonishing green silk cravat was pointing impatiently at three overturned demitasse cups that rested on his small table next to one of the lilac trees. "Come, Rudi, my boy, it's painfully simple. Don't dawdle so."

The small frail waiter hunched, shifted his feet, tugged at his black bow tie, rubbed his perspiring palms once again on his long white apron. "Well, Herr Lorenzo, I think maybe perhaps—"

"My boy, what did I tell you my name was?"

Rudi smacked himself on the temple with the heel of his hand. "Forgive me, my mind was wandering," he apologized. "Well, Herr Great Lorenzo, I think maybe the cube of sugar must be under . . ." His hand, trembling slightly, hovered over the center

cup in the row of three and then darted to the one on
the left. ". . . yes, under this cup."

"Ah, what a pity," sighed the Great Lorenzo.
"You're wrong once again, Rudi, and that makes six
more free brandies you owe me. Plus the five eclairs
from our earlier round of fun."

At a nearby table a handsome red-haired woman
in a satin dress began giggling over something her
thickset gentleman companion had said. Her fluffy
feather boa nearly slipped from her shoulders as she
swayed in her chair.

"Might I," inquired the waiter tentatively, "see
for myself it isn't under there, Herr Loren— Herr
Great Lorenzo?"

"Eh? You doubt my— Ah, but of course. I am a
stranger in your land." The Great Lorenzo fluffed
his graying muttonchop whiskers. "To you I am
merely a wandering minstrel who happens to be
starring, twice nightly, in a magical extravaganza at
the nearby Rupert Theater. Were this America, my
boy, were this my own, my native land, you'd be fully
aware that the Great Lorenzo is a man of unim-
peachable honesty and unassailable integrity. Two
years ago in Chicago, in fact, I was prevented from
running for a prestigious public office on the grounds
that I was simply too honest." Giving a shrug, he
lifted the cup the waiter had tapped.

There was nothing beneath it but crisp white
tablecloth.

"Forgive me, Herr Great Lorenzo, for ever doubt-
ing—"

"Think nothing of it, my lad." The Great Lorenzo
made a dismissing gesture with his plump beringed
right hand. "Now, rather than cringing here and delivering any further tearful apologies, why don't you

instead trot into that inspired kitchen of yours and fetch me the first of my hard-won eclairs, eh?"

"At once, at once, Herr Great Lorenzo."

"Good thing this isn't New York." Harry Challenge sat down opposite the magician. "They'd have given you the heave-ho long ago for trying such an obvious flimflam on—"

"One of the chief advantages of an outdoor bistro, Harry, is that there are no swinging doors to be flung through," observed the Great Lorenzo. "Speaking of which, you look as though you've had the proverbial bum's rush applied to your person not long since."

"I got tossed out of the palace."

"Serves you right for trying to mingle with your betters." The portly magician uprighted the trio of cups he'd been using in his shell game. The sugar cube wasn't beneath any of them. "Since you won't be spending the evening in amorous pursuits, why not, as I earlier suggested, join me for dinner at some—"

"Nope. Believe I'll just head back for the hotel."

"To sulk?"

"I might do a little of that," admitted Harry.

The Great Lorenzo waved his right hand through the air and a bright yellow theater ticket appeared between his fingertips. "Take in my second show at the Rupert, my boy. I'm planning a new variation of sawing a lady in half, and dear Sara may—"

"I've told you a little about the princess, haven't I?"

"A little? When I encountered you last year in Manhattan, you poured gallons of syrupy reminiscences into my sympathetic ear," replied the magician. "Of course, you'd just returned from last year's visit to this jeweled city in the crown of European real estate and were bubbling over with—"

"I was last over here late in the winter of ninety-five," said Harry, puffing absently on his cigar. "A government minister wanted the Challenge International Detective Agency to handle a case for him and my father sent me—"

"How is your dear papa these days?"

Harry frowned. "Ogres usually don't change much," he answered. "At any rate, I met Alicia, she was just twenty-one then and—"

"I know, I know. A great and wondrous romance blossomed, but in the end, alas, duty forced you to return to American shores, and the fair princess, with heavy heart, turned her attentions once again to the demands of her kingdom."

"You make it sound like a dime novel, Lorenzo."

"Everyone's life is a dime novel, my boy," the magician said with a wistful sigh. "It's when one gets to thinking his life is a Shakespearean tragedy that the trouble commences."

A gaggle of some half dozen street musicians, decked out in crimson and gold, went marching lazily down the middle of the narrow street, filling the gaslit air with brassy militant music.

Eventually Harry said, "Maybe I am making too much of all this."

"Would you care to join me in a brandy? Or an eclair?"

"The thing is," continued Harry, "when our agency was hired to escort Mr. Katjang Otak and his crown jewels from New York City to the Burmese Pavilion at the Exposition here, I let myself get the idea I could pick up where—"

"Zevenburg has many another pleasure to offer,

my lad," the Great Lorenzo pointed out. "For example, I am doing two magnificent shows nightly at the very threshold of the Exposition grounds. You're absolutely certain you don't want even one eclair?"

"When I sent in my card tonight," said Harry, "these two louts came out of the damn palace to throw me in the direction of the gutter."

"Are you and your dear old dad still using that business card with the staring eye and the catchy slogan 'A Wide-Awake Detective Agency' emblazoned upon it? That's been known to annoy some otherwise placid individ—"

"Alicia's changed, I guess."

"Her father is said to be at death's door. Perhaps, Harry, that accounts for—"

"Okay, King Ulrich's dying. She could still have sent a short note explaining—"

"Would you like me to introduce you to my assistant, Sara? A charming lass, titian-tressed and quite surprisingly well-read. She can actually recite interminable stretches of Browning," said the helpful magician. "That ability, coupled with her impressive bosom, might well distract you for a bit."

"I've been thinking, Lorenzo, that there's no real reason for my staying in Orlandia at all," Harry said. "The jewels are now safely on display inside the Exposition and—"

"Stay on," advised the Great Lorenzo. "You've hardly even taken in any of the sights and wonders of the Exposition itself."

"Excuse me, Herr Great Lorenzo." The frail waiter was again beside the table, a pale blue envelope held against his narrow chest. "The boy brought this for your friend."

"Which boy?" inquired the magician, glancing around.

"The lad over by the lady with all the feathers in her— Ah, but he seems to have vanished, sir."

With a shrug the Great Lorenzo took the envelope and passed it across the table. "Smells romantic, my boy."

Harry had recognized the handwriting on the envelope face before he even took hold of it. Opening the envelope, he extracted a folded sheet of blue notepaper.

Harry dearest: Please forgive what occurred when you attempted to call. I do want to see you again, but not here. Can you meet me tonight at eleven in the Pavilion of Automatons on the Exposition grounds? I have much to tell you.

Love, Alicia.

The Great Lorenzo drummed his fingers on the table edge. "Ah, how well I remember the last time I received an amorous missive penned upon notepaper with a royal crest. 'Twas in Bosnia nearly a decade ago, shortly after I had introduced my sensational Floating Lady illusion and the whole of the nation was atwitter and agog over my—"

"She wants to see me after all." Harry folded the note, returned it to the envelope.

"At the palace?"

"At the Exposition."

Nodding, the magician said, "Good, the ground is much softer thereabouts. If you get heaved out again, aim for one of the flower beds or a patch of verdant sward. Although—" He ceased speaking, a look of pain suddenly spreading across his plump face.

His chair creaked as he sank back, bringing one hand up to press against his chest.

"What's wrong?" Harry was on his feet.

The magician waved him down. "Nothing, my boy, not a thing." His voice was a bit dim and throaty. He coughed into his hand before continuing. "I keep forgetting I am but a stage illusionist and not a true magician."

Settling back into his chair, Harry slipped the pale blue envelope into the breast pocket of his coat. "You saw something?"

"Nothing at all, no," said the Great Lorenzo. "I have to keep reminding myself I can't really see the future and that these occasional flashes, these unbidden peeks ahead, mean absolutely nothing. Merely, no doubt, the result of mixing eclairs stuffed with clotted cream and rather inferior brandy."

"Your latest vision had something to do with me?"

With a slow sigh his portly friend answered, "If you must know, my boy, I saw you stretched out upon a floor of black and white mosaic tiles. That assignation invitation was clutched in your hand, and there was a handsome sword of some sort thrust into you in the vicinity of your heart."

"Vivid," said Harry, exhaling smoke.

"As I say, not at all a dependable glimpse ahead," the magician assured him. "Don't let me spoil your evening, my boy."

Harry grinned. "Why would your predicting my death spoil my fun?"

"Even so," the Great Lorenzo said, "it wouldn't hurt to be as careful as you can this evening."

Chapter 2

The weather changed a few minutes shy of eleven that evening. A fine, misty rain began to fall, and the thousands of lights of the Exposition grounds became faintly blurred. The music and laughter and the babble of hundreds of excited conversations seemed suddenly muffled, too.

Harry was making his way through the crowd circling the main fountain when the rain started. The two arched dolphins were spouting streamers of purple water, the single naked water nymph was spilling a cascade of gold from her tilted horn of plenty. Cutting through a flower garden and then double-timing along a path of slick white gravel, Harry reached the Streets of Cairo Exhibit just in time almost to collide with a plump matron riding one of the fair's hundred and some white burros.

"Please, whatever you do, don't annoy the brute," the gray-haired Englishwoman pleaded. "Whenever he becomes annoyed, I tumble off."

Grinning and tipping his hat, Harry eased around the woman and her mount. He'd been to Cairo once on a case for the Challenge International Detective Agency and this crooked block-long alley, with its low white houses and mosques, overhanging upper stories and multicolored awnings, looked fairly authentic. But it smelled much better than the real Cairo ever had.

A small ragged Egyptian boy of ten or so thrust a wooden bowl into Harry's midsection as he passed the alcove the boy was huddled in. "Baksheesh," the boy requested.

Harry fished out an Orlandian coin of modest denomination and flipped it into the bowl.

"My mother tell your fortune for—" The boy had stopped talking and was staring up into Harry's face, mouth slightly ajar.

"Aren't you going to finish your sales pitch?"

"It is of no matter." The boy dodged around him. "Don't waste your money, for you have no future." He went scurrying away among the legs of the tourists.

"Damn," reflected Harry as he continued on his way, "people are sure going out of their way to predict dire things for me."

Well, maybe it wasn't all that damn bright to be pursuing Alicia again anyway. She was *Princess* Alicia, after all, and fairly soon she'd be Queen Alicia. Best thing to do would be to forget what had happened between them over a year ago.

That wasn't altogether an easy chore, though. Alicia had been unlike any other woman Harry had ever met. She was beautiful and—

"Dime novel stuff again," he warned himself.

At the end of the Egyptian lane there was a stretch of parklike land, dotted with trees and wrought-iron benches. On the far side of this small park loomed the Pavilion of Automatons, a large building with a domed roof. Its walls were of pale imitation marble, its curving roof was made up of bluish glass panels set in a fretwork of white metal.

The rain fell heavier now. Harry ran when he reached the grassy area.

At the doorway of the pavilion two British seamen were just turning away.

"No use, guv," one of them informed him. "She's closed up for the evenin'."

" 'Ad me 'eart set on seein' that clockwork dancin' girl," muttered his mate.

Turning up the collars of their peacoats, they hurried away.

Harry, frowning, approached the closed metal and stained-glass doors of the darkened pavilion. Affixed to one of the glass panels was a hastily written note.

> *Temporarily Closed.*

Hands in pockets, Harry stood with his back to the door. The rain hit down on the metal awning that sheltered the doorway. There was no sign of the princess anywhere.

Behind him a door creaked and a thin piping voice called out, "We are not closed to you, Herr Challenge."

It took Harry a bit more than ten minutes to determine he was the only living person inside the dimly lit Pavilion of Automatons. He was certain he was sharing the place with just the two dozen clockwork figures arranged in alcoves and upon low pedestals. He'd long since noticed that the floor was made up of black and white mosaic tiles that formed giant serpentine patterns. He reminded himself that Lorenzo's predictions quite often didn't come true.

Nearest the doorway stood the dancing girl the sailors had been anxious to see. She was a little over five feet high, dressed in a spangled Gypsy costume. She was poised on one foot with a tambourine raised high above her kerchiefed head. In the flickering light provided by the two gas lamps that had been left on she looked almost real.

"Almost," said Harry as he began another slow circuit of the long room.

Next to the immobile dancer sat a tiny golden-haired boy clad in a red velvet lace-trimmed suit. On his tiny lap rested a tablet, and he held a quill pen in his pink, pudgy right hand.

There was a clockwork flutist and a fortune-telling old witch, a caged mechanical canary and a juggler. At the far end of the room two life-size young men in fencing costumes faced each other holding sabers.

While Harry was studying the two realistic figures, the dancing girl's tambourine rattled.

He spun.

She didn't appear to have moved.

The only sound he heard was the night rain hitting on the dozens of glass panels high above.

Then he noticed that the feather pen in the little boy's hand was flickering.

Harry went sprinting over there.

The mechanical boy had stopped writing by the time Harry reached him.

Scrawled across the white sheet of paper was a message for him.

Leave Zevenburg. It is not safe for you.

Harry took a step back from the little automaton. Lifting off his hat, he scratched at his dark, curly hair. "Well now, I'll tell you," he said aloud, his voice echoing. "I was aiming on leaving the whole damn country bright and early tomorrow. Now, though, I'm not so sure."

"Too bad, too bad." The old fortune-teller had spoken in a dry, rattling voice. "Now you'll die, now you'll die."

Above the drumming of the rain Harry heard heavy footfalls. He turned to see one of the fencers walking, quite gracefully, toward him. The blade of his saber caught the light of one of the bracket gas lamps and sparkled once.

"Clockwork or flesh and blood," Harry warned the approaching figure, "you're not going to take a slice out of me." He reached inside his coat for his revolver.

The gun was no longer there.

Somebody out in that crowd, the Egyptian beggar kid most likely, was a damn good pickpocket.

Keeping his hand inside his coat, Harry started backing for the doorway. "I'd sure hate to shoot up a valuable piece of machinery like you," he told the swordsman, who was now less than twenty feet from him.

All at once Harry tripped.

He fell over backward, arms flying wide.

The little velvet-suited boy had gotten behind him somehow, unseen and unheard. Making a chittering, giggling noise over what he'd done, the small cherubic automaton went scurrying away into the darkness at the edge of the room.

Before Harry could scramble to his feet, the

swordsman's blade, sharp edge outermost, came
swishing down toward his head.

Harry rolled.

Rolled right into the mechanical man, toppling
him over.

The figure landed hard and made a rattling clang.

Harry dived to his left, got to his feet and ran
for the end of the room. The other fencer was still
unmoving on the pedestal. Harry shouldered the figure off his perch, at the same time grabbing the saber free from his waxen hand.

It was a British-style saber, its blade of finely tem-
pered steel and about an inch shy of being three feet
long. Harry'd been taught to use a saber by his father, starting back in his fifteenth year. Quite probably even a murderous automaton wouldn't be as
nasty an opponent as his father had been.

The mechanical man who was trying to kill him
was upright again, coming slowly his way.

"Might as well make this sporting." Harry saluted
his opponent with his borrowed weapon.

Stopping a few feet short of Harry, the fencing automaton returned the salute. He immediately thereafter launched a running attack.

That was an approach Harry's impetuous father
had frequently favored. He parried the mechanical
man's thrust, retreated and then lunged.

The automaton met the blade of Harry's saber
with a blocking parry and their blades clanked.

Harry prevented his opponent's riposte with an
unorthodox wrist flick. Grinning bleakly, he tried a
running attack of his own. Lunging, he passed his
blade over the point of his adversary's, raised the
other saber and then achieved a touch.

When the point of his saber hit the chest of the automaton, there was a small rattling metallic sound.

His clockwork opponent closed with him suddenly and neither of them could use his blade.

This close Harry could see a faint reddish glow behind the glassy eyes, and he was aware of a faint scent of machine oil.

They moved free of each other and the bout continued. Their blades clicked against each other in the silent shadowy pavilion. The rain was falling hard now, pounding on the blue glass dome overhead.

As he fought the automaton Harry realized something. Although the mechanical man had been built to do a bit of assassination now and then, he was basically only an expert fencer. Expert, but quite traditional and conservative. His parries and ripostes were all by the book.

"No reason for me to get skewered by this gadget," Harry decided. "So let's quit fighting fair."

Grinning more broadly into the waxen face, Harry lunged again and then, unexpectedly, kicked the mechanical swordsman in the crotch.

"Yow!" exclaimed Harry, finding the groin area of the automaton untraditionally hard and unyielding.

Nevertheless, his kick succeeded in knocking the machine man off balance.

Hopping on his pained foot, Harry swung his saber in chopping fashion at the off-balance automaton.

The cutting edge of his saber bit into the face, sending chunks of pink-tinted wax flying. The skull beneath was of polished metal.

Pivoting as the mechanical man attempted to strike him with his blade, Harry executed another kick.

This one caught his opponent in the backside.

The automaton stretched out in the air like an enormous jumping jack. Then he fell over onto the black and white floor.

Harry followed him down, crouching over him and hacking at the wax and metal head with his saber.

The fallen machine man made tinny choking noises, arms and legs starting to jerk convulsively. Then his scalp, dark imitation hair and all, popped clear off his head. The silvery metal top of his skull quivered, swung open and vomited out gears, wires and intricate twists of metal. A small rainbow-tinted pool of oil was spreading swiftly across the mosaic tiles.

Sucking in air, Harry stood back and away from the dead machine.

Glancing around carefully, he made his way to the doorway of the Pavilion of Automatons.

Crouched in the shadows near the doors was the writing boy in the little velvet suit. "We won't forget," he chirped in his small voice. "We won't forget."

"Neither will I," promised Harry.

He was outside in the heavy rain, walking through the Chinese Street, when the stares and murmurs of the damp tourists caused him to realize he was still carrying the borrowed saber.

Harry threw it away in the first flower bed he came to.

Chapter 3

Harry was attempting to concentrate on the front page of the morning paper. There was political unrest in Ruritania, a severe earthquake had struck the farmlands of Graustark, there'd been an assassination attempt in Valeria. He set the newspaper aside and picked up his coffee cup.

Two tables over, a wealthy middle-aged American tourist couple were discussing their itinerary for the day. The woman, plump and muffled in fur and feathers, held a red-covered Baedeker as though it were a hymnbook. There were few other patrons as yet, since the hour was early. The six bright yellow canaries, each in its own gilded cage dangling from one of the gold hooks around the dark-paneled restaurant walls, were singing happily. They were apparently not bothered by the fact that little of the morning sunshine penetrated the heavy shutters of the leaded windows. Illumination in the Hotel Ritz-Zauber's restaurant was provided by a huge crystal chandelier and crystal wall lamps recently converted from gas to electricity. The maroon carpeting was so thick it killed all sound of movement.

The Ritz-Zauber—even Baedeker agreed on this— was one of the best hotels in Zevenburg. Harry didn't

much like the place and found it too frilly and fancy,
yet he always stayed here. His father felt that any
partner in the Challenge International Detective
Agency must always reside in a top hotel. As the
only partner besides his formidable father, Harry
didn't exactly agree, but he didn't argue.

He glanced at the front page once again, then
sipped at his coffee.

" '. . . wet umbrellas and parcels must be left in
the cloakroom,' " the plump American tourist was
reading to her husband. " 'Then one is ready to stroll
along the echoing corridors of the renowned Kunsthistorisches Museum to view the many—' "

"It isn't raining," interjected her small gray husband.

"Well, of course, it isn't, Silas."

"Then why bother to tell me what to do with my
wet umbrella? Seems to me, Fanny . . ."

Harry slid the blue envelope out of his breast
pocket, removed the note he'd received last night.
After unfolding it and spreading it out on the crisp
white tablecloth, he ran his fingertips over the royal
crest at the top of the page. He was damn sure this
was a real sheet of Princess Alicia's notepaper, and
equally certain the handwriting was hers.

She'd written him fifteen letters during his last
visit. And Harry had saved them.

"Schoolboy stuff," he murmured. "A wonder I
didn't tie them up with a pink ribbon."

"I didn't realize I had a hangover until I heard
those nitwit birds," announced the Great Lorenzo as
he settled in opposite Harry. "My own fault, drink-
ing champagne out of the duchess's slipper after our
intimate midnight supper."

Harry slipped the letter away. "Which duchess is this?"

"Duchess Hofnung," replied the portly magician, who was decked out in a bottle-green frock coat and fawn trousers this morning. "A petite, though aging, beauty who is possessed of uncommonly large feet. Her slippers, as a result, held— Cease that vile chirping!" Twisting in his chair, he gestured at the nearest birdcage.

All six canaries fell suddenly mute.

"Nice trick," observed Harry.

"Not a trick, my boy, simply an exhibition of mental telepathy," explained the Great Lorenzo. "Since my brain—my critics and detractors to the contrary —is superior to that of a canary bird, there's no real— Whatever is that plutocrat babbling about?"

The tourist was poking at his plump wife. "Fanny, what's wrong? Why can't you speak? I didn't mean to be snide about the Spaniscue Hofreitschule."

"Ah, a little spillover," realized the magician. "I didn't mean to include you, madam." He snapped his pudgy fingers.

" '. . . no one should miss the lyric singing of the famed Sevenburg Boys' Choir,' " resumed the befurred matron.

The magician said, "One must be most careful not to abuse power. Now, before I regale you with a fiery account of what befell me last evening by simply complying with the hitherto unknown duchess's written request to teach her a few simple card tricks, fill me in, my lad, on your own amorous adventures. What did that mysterious billet-doux lead to?"

Harry drank some of his coffee. "Alicia wasn't there."

The magician blinked. "Not a very auspicious beginning for a tempestuous romance."

"However," said Harry, grinning, "one of the automatons did make a try at killing me. That was right after I was warned to get out of town."

The Great Lorenzo pressed his hand to his waistcoat. "Then my vision was at least partially accurate," he said thoughtfully. "There was death awaiting you at the pavilion last night."

"Yep, and from a sword, too." Harry gave his illusionist friend an account of what had happened to him the previous evening.

When he finished, the magician plucked a Turkish cigarette out of the air and lit it with his fingertip. Exhaling smoke, he said, "Perhaps, my boy, those clockwork gadgets gave you sound advice. As you yourself pointed out last evening, your work in Orlandia is done. Why not journey over to Ruritania or—"

"Nope, not yet."

Clearing his throat, the magician leaned closer to Harry. "Do you have any notion how expensive one of those mechanical men is, my boy? Anyone who would construct one for the sole purpose of doing you in is a blackguard with an impressive budget. He may be willing to spend even more to speed you to your grave, Harry."

"Even so," he said, "I think I'll look into the situation."

"But why? Whether or not the princess sent you the note, there looks to be little chance of rekindling your former romance," his friend pointed out. "I hear, by the way, that Princess Dehra of Valeria is quite a looker and very personable. Why not run over there to—"

"Somebody wants me dead," cut in Harry. "I'd like to know who and why."

"Forgive me, gentlemen, for not hastening to your table sooner," apologized the tall, gaunt waiter who materialized beside their table. "The maître d' had me trying to coax our birds to sing again and thus, sir, I failed to note your arrival until now." He bowed to the Great Lorenzo. "Might I take your breakfast order?"

"I happen to be," the magician told him, "a leading ornithologist. I'm confident I can cure these poor feathered creatures and have them harmonizing in no time."

"You could? How wonderful. What, sir, would be your fee?"

The magician dismissed the notion of money with a lazy wave of his hand. "I would do it simply out of my love for canaries," he explained. "If, however, the management could see its way clear to provide me with a plate of bratwurst and sautéed potatoes, with three fried eggs on the side and a large pot of tea, my good man, I would greatly appreciate it."

The waiter bowed once more. "I am certain that can be arranged, Herr Doctor," he said. "And will you cure them immediately or—"

"Right after my breakfast," promised the Great Lorenzo.

Bowing even more deeply, the gaunt waiter withdrew.

"I probably could've gotten them to toss in a bottle of wine as well," the magician reflected. "Ah, well, a bit early in the day for that." He fluffed his sidewhiskers. "Where was I? Yes . . . Harry, my lad, your wisest course is to leave Zevenburg."

Harry nodded. "Yep, that probably is the smart

course, Lorenzo," he agreed. "However, what I'm actually going to do is dig into this for a couple of days."

"How?"

"Well, first off I'm heading back to that Pavilion of Automatons this morning," he replied. "Take a look at the place in the daylight. Also want to see if I can find that Egyptian beggar boy who more than likely filched my gun."

"Since you no longer have a weapon, Harry, why not—"

"Always carry a spare in my valise." Grinning, Harry patted his shoulder holster.

"I still maintain— But what's this?"

Their waiter was hurrying silently back toward their table across the thick carpeting. He held a yellow envelope. "Herr Challenge, is it?"

"I'm Harry Challenge, yes."

He thrust out the envelope. "A cablegram just arrived for you."

"Thanks." Harry took the envelope and the waiter eased away.

"I hope," remarked the Great Lorenzo while he was opening it, "you're being summoned to come at once to Guatemala or some other lush—"

"From my father." Harry read the message, passed the cablegram to the magician.

Dear son: Get your miserable lazy carcass over to the Grand Imperial Hotel there in Zevenburg. See Jack Mariott and sister. He's hired us. Rich as sin. Don't dawdle. Your devoted father, the Challenge International Detective Agency.

When he finished reading, the magician leaned

back in his chair. "Although this doesn't get you out of town, my lad, it at least will keep you from poking your nose any further into the Princess Alicia matter."

"It would," said Harry, "if I was going to pay any attention to it."

Chapter 4

The morning was bright and clear, and a very gentle breeze drifted across the vivid green meadows and woodland glades of the Volksgarten Park. On the other side of the tree-lined lane a white-suited vendor was selling multicolored ices from an umbrella-shaded cart. When three uniformed college students came speeding by on their bicycles, the tiny brass bell on the cart gave a sympathetic jingle.

Harry, after taking his leave of the Great Lorenzo on the marble steps of the Ritz-Zauber, had cut across the sun-bright park toward the Exposition grounds.

He slowed now and stopped, pretending to be debating whether or not to cross over and buy an ice. Actually he wanted to take a careful look behind him. For the past several minutes he'd again had the feeling he was being tailed.

Two French sailors were sharing a stroll with a giggling blond local girl. A bewhiskered gent was feeding strudel crumbs to some blasé park squirrels. A small, pouting little boy in a velvet suit was being taken for a reluctant walk on a leash by his hefty nanny.

No one else was to be seen behind him at all.

While Harry was standing there an old woman who sold flowers started to cross the road from his side.

"Look out!" cried the vendor.

From around a bend in the road a black stallion came galloping. The man in the saddle was dressed all in black. His face was lean, his dark hair was close-cropped and a puckered white scar snaked across his left cheekbone.

Although the horse was heading right for the flower seller, the dark rider made no effort to rein up or swerve.

Harry had started running while taking all this in.

He reached the old woman, grabbed her by the arm and yanked her back clear out of the charging animal's path.

The rider said, "Swine!" at Harry and kept on his course.

"Hey, you damn fool!" called Harry at the retreating horseman. "You came—"

"No, no, sir. It is nothing, please," whispered the old woman, clutching her basket of flowers closer to her.

"Nothing? That idiot almost—"

"You want no trouble with him." She crossed herself awkwardly, watching the horse and rider gallop out of sight. "That was Dark Otto."

"Was it now?" Letting go of the woman, Harry lifted off his bowler. He dusted it, popped it back atop his head. "Baron Otto Van Horn, huh? Didn't recognize him right off. He's even uglier than he was last time I—"

"You mustn't say that, sir," the flower vendor warned as he guided her across the roadway. "For even though Dark Otto is not in favor with his family, he is a powerful and vindictive man."

"I thought the royal family had an agreement with their black sheep," said Harry. "Otto was supposed to stay at his chateau in the Blackwood Forest and never visit Zevenburg except on rare formal occasions."

"Because our poor monarch is so ill . . ." She made another sign of the cross. "Dark Otto is allowed to breach the rules."

"That's not smart."

"It isn't, no. Yet you ought not to say so." She selected a white carnation out of her wicker basket, handed it to him. "Thank you for helping me, sir."

Grinning, Harry adjusted the flower in his buttonhole. "Thank you for filling me in on the political situation." From his pocket he took a silver coin and dropped it in her basket.

He resumed walking.

Harry had covered another half mile when a closed carriage caught up with him. It was drawn by two handsome gray geldings.

He casually reached inside his coat toward his Colt .38.

"By George, that was quite splendid," called a youthful voice from within the carriage. "The way you snatched that poor creature from the very jaws of death. Smashing."

Harry nodded, saying nothing.

The door of the carriage swung open, allowing him to see a blond young man of about twenty-five, clad in a tweedy Norfolk suit and matching cap. The youth smiled approvingly out at him.

"I'm very impressed," said the blond young man,

"and more than ever convinced we've picked the right man."

"You've picked me for something?"

The young man hit his forehead with the heel of his hand. "I'm going about this backward I fear, forgive me," he said. "Amy's forever pointing that out to me. Should've brought her along, except she's on a shopping tour with a delightful English girl we met on the boat. Stop the carriage, won't you?"

The driver obliged.

The young man hopped lithely free into the morning sunlight. "I'm Jack Mariott," he explained, holding out his hand.

After making certain no one else was going to come popping out of the dark carriage, Harry extended his hand. "Harry Challenge."

"Yes, I know. That's why I've been pursuing you, you see." He shook Harry's hand with vigor before letting go. "Tried to catch you at your hotel, but apparently just missed you. A helpful old gentleman, who seems to have the knack of plucking cigars out of the thin air, suggested I'd find you taking your morning constitutional in the park here. I'm quite fond of exercise myself."

"Actually I'm on my way to a business meeting and—"

"We're most anxious, Amy and I, that you begin working for us at once," said Mariott. "Would a bonus, perhaps, persuade you to drop everything else?"

"I can get over to your hotel first thing tomorrow. The Grand Imperial, isn't it? That way—"

"I am prepared to offer you an additional ten thousand dollars." He reached inside his Norfolk jacket.

Harry took a step back, sizing up his new client. "What fee did you and my father agree on?"

"Twenty thousand dollars," answered Mariott as he took out his wallet. "Reasonable enough, considering the nature of the case and the excellent reputation of your detective agency."

Harry glanced up at a pair of doves on a tree branch overhead. He and his father split everything fifty-fifty. Meaning he'd make fifteen thousand dollars for handling this fellow's case. And if he agreed to drop everything, he'd have ten thousand dollars right now.

Mariott was counting out new hundred-dollar bills. "I only have about two thousand on my person. At the hotel, though, we—"

"Why the rush, Mariott? Couldn't your case wait a day or so until—"

"It is, Mr. Challenge, a matter of life and death."

Harry tapped the pocket that held his father's cablegram. He looked from the hundred-dollar bills to the doves and back again. "Okay," he said, taking charge of the cash. "I'll come along with you now to your hotel."

"Splendid!"

The sommelier had a cold. Every time he sneezed, the gold keys on the gold chain around his neck rattled and clanged faintly. That barely detracted from the overall splendor of the world-renowned Garden Court Restaurant of the Grand Imperial Hotel. The place was immense, accommodating well over one hundred tables. At this hour, a few minutes past noon, every table was filled, and more anxious patrons could be seen crowded behind the plush crimson rope that guarded the main entry. The restaurant interior was two full stories high, covered over with a domed ceiling of white-painted metal and faintly rose-tinted panels of glass. Midday sun was streaming down, filling the interior with light and illuminating the profusion of potted plants and trees that gave the famed dining place its name.

Harry had the feeling he was lunching in a vast greenhouse. "Go on," he urged Amy Mariott.

She was a blond young woman of no more than twenty, pretty, though a shade too plump for Harry's taste. She wore a simple satin frock with a high collar. One of her plump hands rested on the copy of the second volume of the Tauchnitz edition of Anthony Trollope's *Can You Forgive Her?* that she'd been reading when Harry and her brother had joined her.

Amy had paused to glance over at the sneezing wine steward. "Poor man, a dose of sulphur and molasses would fix him up fine," she said. "But I don't suppose they have any in this entire country. You can't help wondering—"

"Amy, you're being discursive," her brother pointed out. "You always accuse me of—"

"Oh, tush," said Amy, feigning a pout. "I can come to the point faster than you any old day, Jack, and not go around Robin Hood's barn doing it."

Four musicians, clad in tailcoats, were mounting the elevated dais in the center of the room. As soon as they were seated, the cellist was hidden from view by a luxuriant banana palm.

"Perhaps I better go ahead and explain to Mr. Challenge why we hired him, Amy, since you—"

"I can do it much better than you, Jack." She gave Harry a brief dimpled smile. "You've no doubt heard, Mr. Challenge, of the Great Boston Tea Company?"

"Most everybody has," he answered. "Fact, I read an interesting article in *McClure's* a few months—"

"That was mostly a lot of radical nonsense," said Mariott firmly.

Harry snapped his fingers. "You're that Mariott family."

"Our uncle, Jonah Mariott," confirmed the girl, "is president and chairman of the board of the Great Boston Tea Company. It's no secret he's a millionaire many times over. Although that wicked magazine story exaggerated the extent of his wealth and influence considerably."

"The point is," added her brother, "after our parents were taken from us in a railroad accident five years ago, we became Uncle Jonah's sole heirs."

"I see," said Harry. "And now somebody's trying to come between you and your uncle's money."

"Marvelous!" Amy clapped her hands. "A very perceptive deduction."

Resting his elbow on a patch of sunlit table, he told her, "You'd be surprised, Miss Mariott, how many similar cases we've handled."

She smiled at him again, a bit longer this time. "It isn't just the money," she said. "Jack and I have a very comfortable trust fund that was thoughtfully set up for us by our dear departed parents. I shan't, though, play the hypocrite and pretend we'd rather Uncle Jonah's money went to that quack doctor than to us."

Harry inquired, "He's involved with someone you believe is a charlatan?"

Amy nodded. "We've met the man, had a very unsatisfactory interview with him at his sanitarium, and there is no doubt in my mind he's a complete and utter fraud."

Harry nodded toward her brother. "Who is the man?"

"He calls himself Dr. Mayerling."

Amy shuddered. "He's residing in a dreadfully bleak castle in the Blackwood Forest."

"That where your uncle is?"

Jack said, "He's been an alleged patient there for the past five months."

Reaching out, Amy took hold of Harry's hand. "We are convinced, Mr. Challenge, that Uncle Jonah is a virtual prisoner in Blackwood Castle."

"How does your uncle view the situation?"

"We haven't been able to see him or communicate with him." Amy increased the pressure on his hand. "The castle lies a day's rail journey from here, near the town of Dunkelstein. Jack and I traveled there last week, shortly after our arrival in Orlandia."

"I must admit," said her brother, "that Dr. Mayerling was very cordial to us. But he insisted our uncle was not yet ready to receive visitors of any kind."

"Imagine that, after we'd traveled all the way from America and I was so dreadfully seasick for days on end."

Harry retrieved his hand from her grasp, used it to scratch at his chin. "I've heard a little something about this Mayerling," he said. "He's gained a reputation among the older and wealthier as being able to make them young again. Is that the pitch he gave your uncle?"

"Dr. Mayerling is subtler than that," said Mariott. "He isn't one of those patent-medicine quacks one finds advertising in the back pages of our popular magazines, promising cures for the most deadly diseases. Oh, no, the doctor merely implies that his rejuvenation process has been known to make certain of his patients feel younger."

Harry glanced from Mariott to his sister. "Why'd you two decide to come over here?"

Mariott answered, "Originally Uncle Jonah was to have stayed at the sanitarium for just four weeks. After nearly two months had elapsed, however, he had yet to return."

"Then we received the most strange and unsettling letter from our uncle," picked up Amy. "He claimed that Dr. Mayerling had changed his life, endowed him with an entirely new point of view. He intended to stay on at that dreadful pile for an indefinite period."

"The letter was authentic?"

"Yes, unfortunately," answered Mariott. "We immediately considered the possibility of forgery, even though the handwriting did appear to be that of our uncle. We consulted our attorneys, and they put us in touch with a well-thought-of professor at Harvard who specializes in such things. He assures us the writing in the letter matches that of the samples we provided."

"You have that letter with you?"

Amy shook her head. "I told Jack we should have brought it, but he—"

"Since it was authentic, I saw no need."

Turning, Harry watched the string quartet play for a half minute or so. "Why'd your uncle decide to come over here in the first place? How'd he hear about Dr. Mayerling and his sanitarium?"

Amy blushed. "We haven't, I fear, been completely candid with you," she admitted. "There was— Well, Uncle Jonah had met a woman, a handsome widow many years his junior, and he started contemplating marriage. Then, when one of his cronies at the Union Club mentioned the supposedly marvelous results Dr. Mayerling was getting, Uncle made a direct inquiry to the doctor here in Orlandia."

"This widow didn't tout him on to the place?"

Jack smiled. "She wasn't, I don't believe, all that interested in a serious relationship with our uncle," he said. "Uncle Jonah, nevertheless, convinced himself that were he to appear a few years younger, he'd have a much better chance of winning her."

"I hesitated to mention the lady," said Amy. "Since I didn't wish you to think we two objected to his marrying again. We'd love to see him happy, even if it meant losing our rightful inheritance."

Harry asked, "Your uncle's been paying Dr. Mayerling's fees himself?"

Amy replied, "Exactly. Not only that, though the fees are outrageously high. No, in the past three months Uncle has also apparently donated an additional two hundred thousand dollars to the sanitarium."

"When we learned this," said Mariott, "we decided to come to Orlandia immediately."

"Our attempt to see Uncle Jonah failed miserably," said his sister forlornly. "We'd returned to Zevenburg from the Blackwood Forest to arrange for passage home, when Jack said, 'By George, what say we hire a crackerjack detective?'" She spread her hands wide, smiling at Harry. The sunlight made her blond hair sparkle. "I do believe, after this delightful interview with you, Mr. Challenge, that we have surely hired the right man for the job."

Harry asked, "How old's your uncle?"

"Oh, we ought to have mentioned that sooner," said Mariott. "He's sixty-six."

"Sixty-eight," corrected Amy. "Uncle likes to shave a few years off his true age. He's sixty-eight."

"You saw him before he left for here?"

"At the dock in Boston," replied Mariott. "We made every effort to dissuade him from making the trip, but to no avail, obviously."

"He was in possession of his faculties?"

"He's not senile, if that's what you mean," said Amy. "At least he wasn't then."

"What exactly do you want me to do?"

Amy straightened in her chair. "Why, we want you to rescue him, of course."

"He may not want to be rescued."

"But he's a prisoner," she insisted. "We *know* that."

"I can go to Dunkelstein, nose around some," said Harry. "I can try to see your uncle. But you have to understand that I can't take him out of there against his will. The government of Orlandia, along with those of several other countries over here, allows us to operate in a limited way within its borders. Kidnapping isn't one of the things they let us do."

Mariott said, "You'll do what you think best, Mr. Challenge."

"We're absolutely certain," said Amy, "that Uncle Jonah would leave that castle if he could."

"Okay, I'll see what I can find out," promised Harry.

"Smashing," said Mariott with a pleased smile. "There's a crack train leaving this evening at seven. I've taken the liberty of arranging a first-class compartment for you."

Harry frowned. "I was figuring on departing tomorrow or—"

"That extra ten thousand dollars," reminded the blond young man, "was to guarantee your giving our case your *immediate* attention."

After contemplating that for a bit, and listening to the string quartet play Mozart, Harry said, "Give me the train ticket."

Chapter 5

The twilight brought rain, a fine misty rain that drifted down gradually through the darkening sky. The echoing platforms of the Zevenburg railroad depot were roofed over with massive canopies of iron and stained glass. Rain drifted down through the spaces between the roofs, the drops glistening as they were caught in the glow of the gaslights and the beam of a hulking train engine.

The Great Lorenzo was bundled in an Inverness cape and his abundant side-whiskers were pearled with rain. "It will be a long, dreary odyssey, my boy," he was saying to Harry. From out of the dusky air he plucked the latest issue of *The Strand* magazine. "You'd best add this to your—"

"Lorenzo, Lorenzo, my adorable *spaetzle*," chided the petite Duchess Hofnung from amid her furs, "don't overload your handsome young detective friend with going-away gifts. He merely travels to Dunkelstein, not the ends of the earth."

Harry, wearing a gray travel suit, was clutching a large wicker basket bursting with fresh fruit, a wreath of yellow roses, a tinned ham, a picnic hamper, an assortment of English language magazines and several newspapers.

"I'm especially curious about these flowers you materialized, Lorenzo," he mentioned, jiggling the floral piece. "Why does the ribbon say 'Farewell to Our Loyal Member'?"

"People oft say farewell when one of their bosom chums departs," replied the Great Lorenzo.

"Your carriage passed the Zevenburg Municipal Cemetery on the way to the station, didn't it?"

Narrowing one eye, the portly magician picked a green and crimson Easter egg out of the air. "Hard-boiled egg?"

"Lorenzo," cautioned the smiling little duchess, "your strapping young comrade has already enough to feed a regiment."

"You never know when you'll want an egg." He deposited it in Harry's fruit basket.

"I appreciate your coming to see me off," Harry told him. "Now I'd better find my damn compartment so I can dump all this—"

"Fritzi, you wait in the carriage for me now," suggested the Great Lorenzo. "I have a few things I wish to discuss with Harry in private, eh?"

"You men. Always secrets, secrets. Worse than chambermaids." Her small blond head emerged from among the furs and she gave Harry a warm, moist, scented kiss on the cheek. "So very pleasant to have met you, Herr Challenge."

"Same here."

"Twenty-two A," said the magician, catching hold of Harry's arm and guiding him along the platform, "is right down here someplace, my boy."

Unlike American trains, those on the Orlandia rail lines had cars with doors on both sides.

Harry's compartment proved to be only a hundred yards from where they'd been standing. "Could you maybe make some of this accumulation disappear again?"

"Nonsense, you'll make use of it all before you arrive at your destination." He opened the door. "I understand, too, that the food on this train is not a gourmet's delight. You'll more than likely have to subsist on fruit and eggs."

Harry unloaded all his bon voyage presents on one of the leather-covered seats. "I appreciate your— What's wrong?"

The Great Lorenzo, pale, was pressing his hand to his chest and grimacing. "That chap in the tweed suit," he whispered.

Harry thrust his head out of the open doorway to look down the platform. A small dark man of about forty was walking briskly away from them. He halted now, opened a first-class compartment door and stepped in. "I see him. Don't know him."

The magician was almost breathing normally again. "Nor I," he said in a voice easing back toward normal. "Yet I had a most uneasy feeling when he passed us by."

"Another premonition?"

Shrugging, the Great Lorenzo readjusted his cape. "Be watchful of him. There's something . . . dangerous about him."

"You don't have to stay until the train pulls out." Harry climbed back into his brown-hued compartment. "The duchess is waiting and—"

"Handsome woman, isn't she? For her age."

"She can't be much more than forty, Lorenzo. That's not ancient, especially since you yourself are pushing—"

"I'll slip in and talk with you for a few moments." Nudging the gifts aside, he sat facing Harry.

Harry pulled the door shut. "One thing," he said. "I don't want you to go poking into what happened to me at the pavilion last night while I'm away. If, when I get back from Dunkelstein, I'm still curious, then I'll investigate the setup. Understood?"

"Perfectly, my boy. You, after all, are the detective, and I merely a humble entertainer." He dug into the fruit basket, selected a golden apple and took a hearty bite out of it. "You put even less faith in my premonitions than I do. Still, I do feel I ought to mention that I've . . . seen a few things since last we met."

"Having to do with what, the Princess Alicia business or my work for the Mariotts?"

Shaking his head, the Great Lorenzo answered, "I'm not certain, Harry. All I know is, I had a very sharp and upsetting flash of you being hunted by a pack of wild dogs. Later I saw you in a coffin. Very ornate one it was, made of bronze and filigreed all around. You weren't dead, though, merely stretched out in the thing."

"That's comforting at least."

"Perhaps yes. Perhaps no. I am not clear as to what these two visions might mean." He noticed the copy of *The Strand.* "Ah, a new Rider Haggard yarn. Might I borrow this, my lad?"

"You can take along the hard-boiled egg, too."

The magician tucked the magazine under his arm. "I wish you well. Contact me as soon as you return." He opened the door and stepped out onto the platform. "And should you need any—"

"Stay right there, don't move for a minute," cautioned Harry all at once.

He ducked, grabbed up one of the newspapers.

Hastily unfurling it, he brought it up in front of his face.

"Creditor?" The magician looked around casually, saw only a slim young woman with freckles and auburn hair striding by. She wore a checkered travel suit and was carrying her own heavy suitcase. "Say, isn't that Jennie—"

"Hush," suggested Harry from behind the shield of his newspaper. "I'd just as well she didn't know I was aboard this particular train."

"Why? Publicity never hurt anyone."

"Is she out of range yet?"

"Climbed into a compartment two coaches ahead of yours. Very trim ankle the lass possesses, by the way," said his friend. "That was Jennie Barr, the daredevil girl reporter of the New York *Daily Inquirer,* was it not?"

"Yep, that's her." Slowly he lowered the paper, but kept it ready in his lap.

"She wrote a rather perceptive article about my last show in New York. Taken from the unusual angle of—"

"She's continually trying to poke her damn nose into the agency's business."

"A pretty nose it is."

"Maybe so, but a detective agency wants privacy, not notoriety."

"Come, my boy, neither Pinkerton nor Burns shares your view."

"Well, neither of those gents happens to be my father," Harry pointed out. "He hates publicity, and I'm not all that fond of it myself. So I prefer to avoid Jennie Barr."

"Pity, since she's a bright and comely lass."

"Train'll be pulling out any minute now, Lorenzo."

"I doubt that, since an Orlandian train hasn't left or arrived on time since right after the thaw of ninety-four."

"Even so."

"The hint is perceived and acted upon." He rotated his palm once and another hard-boiled egg, purple and silver this time, appeared. He dropped it into the fruit basket. "Want some salt?"

"No, don't conjure up any. Just close the door and let me lie low until the train's out of the station."

"I seriously doubt you can avoid the young lady from here to Dunkelstein."

"I'm sure going to try."

"I'll wager you won't succeed." He chuckled, tipped his slouch hat and went strolling away down the platform.

Harry pulled down the shades on all the windows of his compartment. "Wonder what the hell Jennie's doing on this train."

Chapter 6

An hour out of Zevenburg, rolling swiftly across flat farm country, Harry's train ran into a storm. The full moon suddenly vanished from the night sky, massive black clouds closed in and hard rain began to pelt the train.

Outside his compartment window, Harry saw an image of himself floating. The rain sliced at it, and when lightning sizzled across the fields of grain, the reflection thinned and was gone. Lights of farmhouses flickered far off in the wet darkness. Another flash of lightning showed him a bareheaded boy riding a white mare hell-for-leather for a great yawning barn.

There were several deep rumbles of thunder, drowning the clacking of the train wheels.

Then Harry saw a second figure floating out there in the rain-swept night.

He spun to face the corridor door, hand diving beneath his coat for his gun.

"I knocked," said Jennie Barr on the threshold.

Bringing out his hand empty, Harry told the reporter, "I have nothing to say to the press."

"Malarkey." She came on in, shutting the door behind her, and settled on the other seat amid his scat-

49

tered gifts. She tucked her legs under her, grinned at him.

She really was a very attractive young woman, twenty-six years old, slender, with pale reddish hair and a light dusting of freckles. She wore the checkered skirt of her traveling suit and a puff-sleeved white blouse, and she was carrying a shoulder bag.

Harry said, "I was hoping you wouldn't find me on board."

Jennie laughed. She had her auburn hair pulled back and held with a tortoise-shell comb. "You get yourself seen off by a half-baked magician who's all but pulling rabbits and pigeons out of his sleeves and you expect to be inconspicuous?"

"Lorenzo's a friend of mine, old friend. Naturally he—"

"I wouldn't mind being your friend, Harry, except—" Her pretty nose wrinkled. "You must have noticed, being a fairly astute detective, that many kids grow up to resemble their parents."

"I have, yes."

"Settling down with you might be fun for a while," she told him as the lightning crackled outside. "The hitch is, see, you'll probably end up being a dead ringer for that crusty old father of yours. Who'd want that?"

"Never having met your folks, I can't—"

"I never did either. I'm an orphan."

Harry watched her for a moment. "Left on a doorstep in a basket pretty much like that one there?"

When Jennie shook her head, a strand of hair fell free. "My parents, whoever they were, apparently couldn't even afford a basket. They delivered me to the steps of a Detroit orphanage in an old faded flour sack. Even so, I managed to look quite sweet, so the sisters later informed me."

"This is bringing tears to my eyes."

"Hard-as-nails Harry Challenge." From her shoulder bag she extracted a stenographer's notebook and a stub of pencil. "Well, enough smart chatter, Harry old pal. I'm after—"

"No interviews."

"Malarkey. You might as well talk to me, since I already know you're going to Dunkelstein. It figures that—"

"How'd you find out where I was heading?"

"By batting my eyes at the conductor. You ought to try it, simpler than using brass knuckles to get information out of people."

"Jennie, a detective is sort of like a priest or a doctor. He takes a vow of—"

"Mother O'Malley!" She laughed aloud, shaking her head. "A little more of that, Harry dear, and I'll expect to see a halo sprout right over your head."

"C'mon. We've run into each other enough in New York for you to know I don't believe in—"

"I know your grouch of a father doesn't like the press, but then he doesn't like kittens and puppy dogs either."

Out in the corridor chimes sounded. "Last call for dinner."

Harry stood up. "I haven't eaten yet."

Jennie stood up. "Thank you, Harry. I'd be delighted to dine with you."

As they moved along the swaying corridor to the dining car, the small dark man in the tweed suit came toward them.

He didn't seem especially dangerous or formidable, although Harry noted a nasty look to his small gray eyes.

The man smiled at Jennie in a nervous, quick way. "Good evening, Fräulein Barr."

"Evening, Mr. Gruber." She pressed back against a carriage wall to let him go shuffling by.

"Know him?" inquired Harry, opening the dining car door for her.

"Name is Gruber. He's a traveling salesman in cutlery. He introduced himself to me this evening earlier when, so he claimed, he entered my compartment by mistake."

"Lorenzo didn't take a fancy to him either."

A plump waiter with a handsome yellow moustache escorted them to a table beside a dark, rain-washed window.

"Oh, does your magic friend know Gruber?"

Harry said, "Noticed him on the platform and . . ." He paused, grinned. "Lorenzo has premonitions sometimes."

"Second sight. Sister Patricia had that, at the orphanage." She picked up the small menu. "Although you don't have to be a mind reader to tell that Herr Gruber's an unsavory character. The sauerbraten sounds good."

Harry had his menu in his hand, but he was looking out the window. Great forks of blue lightning were dancing across the immense darkness of the sky. "I should have Lorenzo along. He's very good at conning people out of free meals."

"Sports editor friend of mine does admirably with a trained cockroach." She dropped her bag on the empty chair next to her. "Now shall we talk about Dr. Mayerling?"

Harry opened his menu. "Might as well," he said finally.

"I won't, since I'm your dinner guest, take notes."

"You're going to Dunkelstein on account of the good doctor?"

Jennie replied, "I suspect he's a confidence man and nothing more. There's no evidence he attended any legitimate medical school in Europe, England or America within the past thirty years."

"And he's been fleecing a number of wealthy Americans."

"Right, exactly. That's the angle that appealed to my editor. Is Dr. Mayerling taking advantage of our gullible native aristocrats? Who is this mystery man who does business out of a haunted castle? Since I was coming over to Orlandia to cover the Exposition anyway, we decided—"

"Is Blackwood Castle supposed to be haunted?"

Jennie shrugged one shoulder. "To *Daily Inquirer* readers all European castles are haunted," she answered. "Besides, with a name like that, it's bound to be cluttered with spooks."

Harry said, "What do you know about Mayerling's persuading his patients to donate substantial sums, above and beyond their treatment fees, to him and his sanitarium?"

"That's one of the items I'm going to be looking into. Now suppose *you* tell *me* something."

"Can't give you the name of my client," he said. "So let's just say I'm working for someone who's concerned about one of Mayerling's patients. And with whether or not this patient is staying at the castle voluntarily."

Nodding, Jennie reached into her bag. "That's another of the rumors about Dr. Mayerling I in-

tend to investigate." She produced her notebook,
flipped it open to a middle page. "Let's see now. I
have the names of the following rich Americans
who are presently residing within the castle. Mrs.
Esme Watt-Evans, Colonel Evan Marshall, Mr.
and Mrs. Melvin Shestack, Ogden Whitney III,
Jonah Mariott, Daphne St. Claire and Hugh S.
Scott." She shut the book. "Your eyes flickered
only on Mariott's name. Is he the one you've been
hired to extricate from Dr. Mayerling's clutches?"

"Jennie, it's one of those on your little list. That's
all I can tell you right now."

The freckled reporter smiled. "I have contacts in
Dunkelstein," she told him. "I'm darn good at finding out things, as you already know, Harry. Be much
more sensible for us to team up and—"

"Nope, I've heard about your idea of teamwork.
Gent on the Chicago *Tribune* mentioned the time on
a steamboat on the Hudson when you were supposed—"

"Heck, that was with another reporter," she said
defensively. "Nobody expects you to play fair with
your own colleagues, not in the newspaper game.
You're different, though. You're a detective and not
a journalist, so I'd play fair with you. On top of
which, Harry dear, we're friends."

"Be that as it may, I am going to work alone. Solo.
Without you."

Her smile returned, broader. "Okay, pretend to
yourself that's the way things are going to be," she
said. "I intend to win you over before we even
reach—"

"Excuse me for intruding," said the yellow-mous-
tached waiter. "I don't like to interrupt a young couple so obviously enamored with each other, yet I

must inform you the kitchen will close very soon now."

Jennie said, "I'll have the sauerbraten."

"The same," said Harry.

"Alas, my heart grows heavy," sighed the waiter. "We're all out of sauerbraten."

Chapter 7

By midnight the train was chuffing its way through the Schweigen Mountains. Thunder rumbled, echoing across the dark chasms, and rain lashed at the windows of Harry's compartment.

Absently he peeled the colorful shell from one of the hard-boiled eggs. "Wish Jennie was off chasing a story in another part of the world altogether," he said to himself.

But did he?

He returned the egg to the basket. Restless, he stood up, shrugged back into his jacket and left the compartment.

The corridor was empty, dimly lit. The sound of snoring came from several of the rooms he passed. Harry moved quietly through the rattling train, heading for the smoking car at the tail end.

The smoking car was empty, thick with stale grayish air. Only one wall lamp was lit, making a cone of light in the middle of the car.

Harry sat down in a tufted armchair beneath the lamp and took a cigar from his breast pocket. He held it in his hand unlit.

You could really hear the rain back here, drumming on the roof and slamming at the windows.

Harry slouched in the chair.

"Let's consider Jennie first," he said inside his head. "Was she really sent out here to do some newspaper articles on Dr. Mayerling?"

Or had the reporter somehow gotten wind of the fact that the Mariotts had hired him? Was she just tagging along to see what he came up with?

"And what about those blond Mariotts?"

Could any two people, especially now in the waning years of the nineteenth century, really be so clean-cut and innocent? They could very well be fakes, ringers, sent by somebody who wanted to get him out of Zevenburg.

"But Jack Mariott's paid me ten thousand dollars in cash," Harry reminded himself. "Be a lot cheaper just to kill me."

That had been tried already, though, at the Pavilion of Automatons last night. They'd failed and maybe decided to just buy him off the scene.

Lord knows, enough people were aware that he, like his father, was mercenary as hell. Money could sure be used to lure him.

"That would mean, then, that this all has to do with my trying to call on Alicia."

Why would that be so damn important? Worth maybe ten thousand dollars, worth killing him for.

Their romance was over. Alicia would soon be the ruler of the country. That would put more than enough barriers between them.

"And what exactly do I really feel about her? A year ago I was sure—"

Someone else had entered the shadowy smoking car. A figure was standing just beyond the circle of light cast by the oil lamp.

"Evening," said Harry, eyes narrowing. "Mr. Gruber, isn't it?"

Gruber edged nearer, smiling ruefully. He had bad teeth. "You'll forgive me, Herr Challenge," he said in his thin nasal voice.

"This car's open to anyone."

Gruber rubbed his hands together. "I meant about what I have to do." He shuffled closer to Harry.

"Selling knives and forks isn't all that bad."

Gruber's quick laugh was like a bark. "Oh, that was a lie. Told to a pretty fräulein."

"Trying to impress—" Harry noticed the man was barefooted. "Sent your shoes out to be shined, did you?"

"I find it helps if I'm not wearing shoes when it happens," he explained, rubbing his hands more vigorously. "The first times, many years ago when I was young, I left them on and it was painful. So now I . . ." The sentence blurred and shifted into a snarl.

Gruber's shoulders were shrugging spasmodically, and he was crouching lower and lower. The lips were pulling back from over his jagged teeth, his nostrils were flaring.

Bristles of dark hair began to sprout on his face. Not just where a beard ought to be, but everywhere. His cheeks, his low forehead, his ears. His jaw seemed to be growing, and his nose and mouth were changing. When he brought his hand up to scratch at his face, it was more a paw than a hand now.

Harry had left the chair. He took three steps back and then reached for his shoulder holster. "Wouldn't advise you to try anything foolish, Gruber." He drew out the Colt .38.

Gruber's only answer was a snarling roar. Teeth bared, he leaped straight at Harry.

* * *

In Zevenburg the Great Lorenzo had concluded his second magic show of the evening a few minutes shy of midnight. Here in Orlandia he liked to finish with his new and improved version of his famous Floating Lady illusion.

He caused his handsome assistant Sara, who was clad in a scant costume of white satin, to seemingly rise high above the dark stage in a rigid horizontal position.

Then the magician reached beneath his scarlet-lined black cape to produce a pistol with a long fili-greed silver barrel. He paused for an instant to cast a fond glance up at Duchess Hofnung in her box.

"Dear ladies and gentlemen of the audience," he announced while taking aim at the floating lady, "let us see if we can bring this lovely creature down to earth again."

He fired two sudden shots at the figure of the young woman. The attentive audience gasped.

Sara vanished in a great cloud of purplish smoke, and a small shower of rose petals fell down, gently, to. the stage.

As enthusiastic applause broke out the Great Lorenzo bowed across the footlights. Then the heavy velvet curtain fell and hid him from view.

Straightening up, the magician hurried back-stage. He was anxious to change and then escort the duchess to a quiet supper at—

The Great Lorenzo slackened his pace. He came to a stop beside a prop table. His left hand, over which he seemed to have lost control, grabbed up the magic slate he'd used earlier in his show.

His right hand picked up a stick of yellow chalk and scrawled a message across the slate.

Shaking his head, as though just awakening, the portly magician held the slate at arm's length to see what he had written.

As regards Harry. It all ties together.

"Not a very impressive handwriting," muttered the magician as he reread the message.

"What's wrong, Lorenzo?" Sara, wearing a Japanese dressing gown over her scant costume, had just come up from the below-stage area where the trapdoor had deposited her just before the dummy replica had gone rising upward.

"Eh?"

"You look somewhat pale and shaken. Are you mooning over that scrawny duchess?"

"Fritzi is petite, not scrawny," he corrected. After taking one last look at the message, he rubbed the slate clean with a red silk handkerchief.

"Your hand's shaking a bit," noticed his assistant. "Remember that time in Graustark when we were playing the Royal Theater and you came down with the grippe? It started exactly this—"

"Fear not, child." He patted her on the shoulder. "I'm not ailing. It does appear, however, that I'm going to have to break my vow to Harry and do a bit of investigating."

Chapter 8

The wolfman had foul breath, a mixture of stale wine and decay. His initial leap knocked Harry over.

Harry's head hit against the claw-footed leg of a chair as Gruber landed atop him.

He snarled and snapped, trying to get at Harry's throat with his teeth.

Straining, Harry brought up his knees and dealt the wolfman a heavy blow in the crotch.

Gruber howled in pain, momentarily preoccupied.

Harry rolled free of him, rose to his knees. He aimed his .38 revolver at the wolfman. "Back off or I'll use this."

Growling, Gruber lunged again. His paws raked at Harry.

Harry fired.

Again.

Twice more.

The bullets thudded into Gruber's shaggy carcass. But they failed to stop him, or even slow him much.

He managed to get a grip on Harry's neck, struggled to sink his jagged teeth into Harry's flesh.

Blood was coming out of the bulletholes in Gruber's tweed coat and rumpled white shirt. The blood was reddish muddy stuff, and it was dripping onto

Gruber's furry hands, matting the thick hair. Yet he didn't seem bothered by the wounds at all.

Harry broke the wolfman's grip on his neck, swung his pistol up. He shot Gruber smack between the eyes.

The bullet bored clean through Gruber's head. Tufts of fur, splotches of blood, fragments of bone and brain went flying, splattering the rose-patterned wallpaper of the swaying smoking car.

The wolfman was unfazed. He was growling deep in his chest, still intent on tearing into Harry's throat.

Harry wasn't in favor of that. Gritting his teeth, he shoved hard at Gruber's chest with both hands.

He succeeded in getting him up and off.

While Gruber was tottering, Harry grabbed an unlit lamp off a table and swung it at the wolfman.

The lamp connected with his muzzle, hard enough to smash the glass and splash oil.

"Stay clear of him, Harry!"

Two pistol shots followed.

Gruber stretched up straight, as though he'd suddenly decided to try to leap up and see if he could touch the ceiling. "No, this isn't—" he said in a bloody, bubbling voice.

The life went sighing out of him. He dropped, knees first, to the floor. Then he pitched over onto the shattered lamp and was still.

"Much obliged," said Harry after taking a deep breath.

Jennie Barr dropped her .32 revolver back into her shoulder bag. "I thought you might need a little help."

"How come your gun brought him down and mine didn't?"

She smiled. "Don't you know, Harry dear, you need silver bullets to kill a werewolf?"

Harry opened his smallest suitcase. From within it he took out a bottle of brandy and two small metal cups. "I told you you should've stayed inside."

Jennie was standing near the window of his compartment, examining the wet splotches on her ankle-length skirt. "I've never seen anyone toss a dead wolfman off the back of a moving train during a thunderstorm before," she said. "I didn't want to miss it."

After pouring brandy into both cups, he handed her one. "Thanks again for saving my life, Jennie."

"Cheers." She clicked her cup lightly against his. "I imagine you'd do the same for me. Wouldn't you?"

He narrowed his left eye. "Probably."

"I think we did the right thing, disposing of Gruber and cleaning up as much of the mess as we could." Sitting down, she took a sip of her brandy.

"Dead wolfmen are tough to explain to the authorities." He settled opposite her.

"Some people maintain a dead lycanthrope will revert to his human form a few hours after death," she said. "That, though, would be even tougher to explain."

"Jennie," he said, watching her freckled face, "how did you happen to have a gun loaded with silver bullets?"

She patted her bag. "Always prepared, that's my motto. I also carry a bottle opener, a skate key, a sewing kit, a compass and—"

"C'mon, don't treat me like one of your newspaper colleagues. Did you know Gruber was going to change?"

"Not him specifically, no," she replied. "See, Harry, I had a hunch Herr Gruber was up to no good. When I just happened to spot him go skulking out of his—"

"Just happened?"

"Well, I guess the fact I was sort of spying on him helped me some." She drank a bit more of the brandy. "I followed him, saw him transform himself to attack you and . . . came to the rescue."

"That still doesn't explain the silver bullets."

She glanced toward the window. "Storm's quieting down," she said. "Well, Harry, I didn't tell you absolutely everything at dinner exactly."

"For one thing, you know a lot more about Dr. Mayerling, don't you?"

"Some," she admitted. "I really do have informants in Dunkelstein. One in particular, a brilliant old gentleman who's an expert on things occult, has given me a lot of information. It's possible, Harry, that the doctor is a lot more than just a quack and a confidence man. He's probably a sorcerer or worse."

"That's impossible, Jennie."

She smiled at him. "How about werewolves, are they impossible, too?"

Harry answered, "Always thought so. Until tonight." He shook his head. "Okay, was Gruber in cahoots with Mayerling?"

"Not certain, though it seems darn likely," Jennie said. "Dr. Mayerling surrounds himself with some very strange associates at that castle of his."

"But he is conning his patients out of money?"

"Yes, but I believe that's mostly to finance his work, his other work."

"Which is?"

She shrugged her left shoulder. "He's supposedly interested in immortality. In carrying on the work of gents such as St. Germain and Cagliostro."

Remembering his cup of brandy, Harry drank most of it down. "If Gruber was working for Mayerling, then it's the doctor who's been wanting me dead."

She eyed him. "Sounds like this wasn't the first attempt."

"Back in Zevenburg," he said. "There was— Hell, Jennie, all of this sounds incredible. At any rate, somebody rigged one of those fencing automatons at the Exposition to come at me. With a saber."

She blinked. "That's . . . bizarre, isn't it?"

"Yep," he agreed. "First a mechanical man, then a werewolf. Beats most anything I ever encountered in the States."

"Orlandia is a very old, and fairly mysterious, country," Jennie said. "You've never met Dr. Mayerling?"

"Not under that name," he said. "Hell, I didn't even know myself I was going to be involved in investigating him when the first attempt was made."

"It might be all this has something to do with your celebrated romance." Standing, she handed him her cup.

"What celebrated romance?"

"The one with Princess Alicia last year. You must be aware it was gossiped about all over the place."

Harry said, "Hadn't occurred to me, no."

"I'm turning in." She eased to the door. "What about my suggestion we team up?"

"I'm considering it," he said. "Seriously."

"Good night, then." Raising up, she kissed him briefly on the lips. "Yell if you need any more help." Smiling, she let herself out of his compartment.

Chapter 9

On tiptoe the Great Lorenzo made his way across alternate stripes of sunlight and shadow toward the carved wood door of the duchess's vast bedchamber.

While he was still several yards from making his getaway, the small marble and gold clock on her dressing table began to chime the hour.

"Renzo, my darling Renzo, wherever are you sneaking off to, fully dressed and all?" called the Duchess Hofnung from the fourposter far across the room.

"Fritzi, m'love," he said, turning to face her, "I have some serious business to take care of."

She was sitting up in bed, arranging her lace negligee and pouting. "So serious you must sneak off before breakfast with me?"

"It has to do with my friend Harry Challenge."

"Ah, your handsome young detective friend? Is he in trouble?"

"He may be soon, my pet, unless I cease dawdling and find out who—"

"Very well, go then, dear Lorenzo." She made a dismissing gesture with her small right hand. "You may use Bruno and the carriage if you wish."

"This task calls for a certain amount of secrecy."

He headed for the exit. "Racing around in a gilded carriage pulled by two white stallions with plumes is not the most subtle way to get about town. Thank you, my sweet, for the offer all the same." He plucked a dozen red roses out of the air, flung them in the general direction of the bed.

While she was still clapping her hands with delight, he made his escape.

The Great Lorenzo took an indirect route across the sprawling Exposition grounds toward the Pavilion of Automatons. He wanted to be absolutely certain not a soul was interested in his activities.

He strolled, swinging his gold-headed cane, along the American Street, and even paused at the simulated soda fountain to buy an ice cream cone. Then he toured the Lusitanian Pavilion and admired the jewels and relics therein.

Quite a few people in the midday crowds recognized him, since his show was a popular one, yet no one seemed to take an undue interest in him.

He wandered slowly along the Cairo Street but couldn't spot the beggar boy Harry had mentioned. A fresh-scrubbed goat nuzzled him when he paused to scan a pottery vendor's wares.

The sign pasted to the door of the Pavilion of Automatons read:

> *Closed Until Further Notice. Sorry.*

After scratching at his two chins with the head of his cane, the Great Lorenzo unscrewed the head and glanced discreetly around.

No one in sight.

He plucked a lockpick out of the hollow head of the cane and used it deftly on the simple lock of the doors.

Inside, while reassembling his cane, he took a slow careful look around.

There was no evidence anything unusual had ever occurred here. Down at the other end there were once again two fencing automatons standing stiffly, facing each other.

Nodding to himself, the Great Lorenzo studied the floor at his feet. "Exactly the pattern I saw in my vision," he confirmed.

Swinging his cane, he started along one row of still, silent mechanical figures.

He halted in front of the cherubic boy with pen and tablet. The topmost sheet was blank. Squatting, puffing, the magician looked the little figure straight in his dead glass eyes. "Any messages, my little man, you'd like to pass on?"

The mechanical boy remained motionless.

"They are lifelike, aren't they? I don't blame you for talking to him."

Lorenzo straightened and slowly pivoted.

Standing in the doorway was a girl dressed in a simple skirt, white blouse and kerchief. Her hair was a pale blond, worn in two braids. She was twenty or twenty-one.

"Were you looking for something, my child?"

Timidly, she crossed the threshold. "I am looking for someone, yes," she answered. "When I saw you unlock the doors, I assumed you must be an official of some sort. Is that so, sir?"

After clearing his throat he said, "In a manner of speaking, yes."

She sighed, smiling. "Ever since I arrived last

night I have had a very difficult time, trying to find anyone who is directly connected with the Pavilion of Automatons." She walked slowly across the mosaic tile floor. "I am Helga Spangler, of Munich." She watched his plump face hopefully.

"Spangler . . ." He tugged at his side-whiskers. "Spangler . . . Ah, would you, dear child, be the daughter of Wolfgang Spangler?"

"I am, yes." She gave a relieved laugh. "Then you do know where he is."

"He's not in Munich?"

Helga's smile vanished. "When you said you knew him, I thought . . ." She began, quietly, to cry.

"I know of him, Helga," explained the Great Lorenzo. "Anyone in my line of work quite naturally has heard of your gifted father. Without doubt Wolfgang Spangler is the best builder of automatons and clockwork figures in all of Europe."

"In all of the world," she amended. "That's why he was sent for, brought here to Orlandia. Over five months ago, to work on these exhibits . . ." Sniffling, she began to walk by the row of figures. "Yes, most of these are his work and yet . . ." She shook her head, her braids flickering. "They're not exactly his work either."

"Am I correct in assuming your father is missing?"

"Yes," she answered. "At least, I believe so. We haven't heard from him in over four months. As soon as I was able, I came here to see what had happened to him."

"What have you found out so far?"

"Only negative things," said Helga. "I went first to the rooming house, which is located on the Nussdorferstrasse, where my father was supposed to have been staying. They maintain he never lived there, that they have no knowledge of him whatsoever."

"And the officials of this Exposition?"

Her shoulders hunched forlornly. "The few I've been able to talk to have offered little help," the girl replied. "One or two say they may have seen my father, months ago when the Exposition was being built, but they have not the slightest idea where he might be at present."

Scratching his chins with the head of his cane, the magician asked, "What of the gentlemen who are in charge of this particular pavilion?"

"I haven't been able to find any of them. This exhibit was suddenly closed down a few days ago and no one knows exactly why."

The Great Lorenzo said, "Do you know who hired your father in the first place?"

"Oh, yes," she said, nodding. "His name was Sir Andrew Mainwaring, a very wealthy Englishman. He offered my father such an impressive fee that he did not feel he could refuse."

"Did the money actually arrive?"

"Yes, half of the amount was paid in advance and most of that is safely in our bank in Munich."

The magician commenced pacing, down as far as the old crone fortune-teller and back. "This must tie in as well," he said, mostly to himself. "Yes, it has to. The missing Spangler, the automaton assassin, Harry's investigation of Dr. Mayerling—"

"Beg pardon, sir?"

He halted beside her. "Do you have a place to stay in Zevenburg, my child?"

"At an inexpensive hotel on the other side of—"

"No, won't do. I want you someplace safe where

you can be looked after," he told her. "Yes, we'll have the dear duchess put you up in one of her guest rooms. She's got dozens of them, each more rococo than the next."

"A duchess? I don't under—"

"Allow me to introduce myself, Helga." He plucked a large business card out of the air and passed it to her. "I am none other than the Great Lorenzo."

Frowning slightly, the girl looked from the boldly engraved card to the magician. "I'm afraid I've never heard of—"

"Never heard of me? Incredible, since we played to sold-out houses for seven weeks in Munich as recently as eight years ago."

"Oh, you are that sort of magician then. A stage magician and not a true one."

"That remains to be seen," he said, fluffing his whiskers. "Come along now, we'll get you installed in Fritzi's menage."

"You intend to help me find my father?"

"Yes, most certainly," he assured her. "I make it a practice to help young damsels in distress, especially when their problems are linked up with mysterious cases I am already investigating." Producing a dozen yellow roses and handing them to the girl, he guided her to the doorway.

Chapter 10

Harry stepped out of his compartment and nearly bumped into what appeared, at first glance, to be an ambulatory bouquet of white roses. "Oops," he said, halting in the brown-carpeted corridor.

"We've got something of a problem," said Jennie, who was carrying the enormous array of roses. "I brought this down to show you."

"Is Lorenzo around?"

"No, this is— Take a look at the card."

Locating the buff card attached to the green paper that shrouded the dozens of flowers, Harry read the inscription, which was written in a bold, clear hand, aloud. " 'To a fine girl and a splendid fellow journalist! Ever, Peter.' "

"Did you happen," inquired the young woman, lowering the huge bouquet enough to look over its top at him, "to hear an enormous thud while we were halted at Froschstadt around dawn?"

"Nope, must've slept through it. Why?"

"That was Peter."

"Doing what?"

The car vibrated as the train went speeding around a woodland curve.

"They were hooking his private car on to the

end of our train." She decided to drop the flowers, propping them against the wall. "Peter Starr McMillion."

Putting his hands in his trouser pockets, Harry gazed up at the swaying ceiling for a few seconds. "The soldier of fortune of the newspaper world? England's answer to Richard Harding Davis?"

"That Peter Starr McMillion, yes. The man who disguised himself as a desert tribesman to interview Sheik Mirhad Waraq, et cetera, et cetera."

"Is he pursuing you or a story?"

"Possibly both," she replied, kicking at the bouquet, tentatively, with her button-shoed foot. "With Peter, though, you can bet the story is at the top of his list."

"And that story must be the same one you and I are interested in?"

"Afraid so, Harry. He's bound for Dunkelstein. Odds are he's interested in Dr. Mayerling's doings."

Taking her arm, he escorted her into his compartment and shut the door. It was late afternoon, and the forest they were speeding through was filling with shadows.

Harry said, "From what I've heard of McMillion, he'll use both fair means and foul to make sure he gets to a story first."

"He will," she said, sitting. "But he really does seem to be fond of me. I mean to say, Harry, Peter's never tried to seduce me off a story."

"Far as you know," he grinned, "and he is a handsome devil."

"Malarkey," she responded, nose wrinkling. "He's Charles Dana Gibson's idea of a handsome fellow. Most women prefer more unconventional faces, such as yours."

"Who's McMillion working for?"

"Most likely the London *Graphic,* although he's also been doing exposés, very polite ones, for the *Gentleman's Monthly.*"

"If it's the *Graphic,* he's got Sir Rollo Shestack's money behind him."

Jennie nodded. "Plus his own family money. I imagine Peter's paying for the private railroad car out of his own pocket," she said. "Did I ever tell you what sort of gift he sent me while he was trying to find the headwaters of the Orinoco River with the Sheepstone Expedition?"

"A shrunken head," answered Harry.

"I did tell you before?"

"Nope, I deduced."

Jennie folded her hands. "He knows I'm going to Dunkelstein; he's probably found out about you, too," she said. "Oh, and he's traveling with a loathsome man who's part valet and part thug. Name of Tubbs and quite handy with a blackjack."

"Amazing the variety of interesting people one meets traveling." Harry fished his watch out and consulted it. "We aren't due to arrive in Dunkelstein for another two hours yet. It's already growing admirably dark."

"What are you contemplating, Harry dear?"

"His car is hooked on to the rear of our train?"

"Just behind the smoking car where we had such fun with the late Herr Gruber, yes."

"Has McMillion invited you to join him in the dining car for tea?"

"Matter of fact, he has. By way of a note that came along with that ton of roses. He suggests we meet in a half hour."

"Accept," Harry told her. "Only tell him you can't

make it for an hour. Send a note, don't go anywhere near his car yourself."

It was raining in Dunkelstein, a heavy, determined rain that slapped down hard on the roof of their horse-drawn carriage. The town was a quaint one, old-fashioned, its two- and three-story houses and shops leaning close together and possessed of slanting red tile roofs, ornately carved shutters and trimmings, colorful chimneys that tilted at odd angles. Rainwater coursed along tile drains, came splashing down on the winding cobblestone streets.

Jennie sat close to Harry, a plaid lap robe over her knees. "Wherever did you acquire a knack like that?" she was asking while plucking the petals from a single white rose.

"States, out West," he answered. "Back almost ten years ago, from my father. It isn't all that difficult."

"And Peter won't be hurt?"

Harry shrugged. "Seems unlikely."

Jennie laughed. "It seems somewhat cruel." She laughed again. "Uncoupling his private car, setting it adrift as it were, while poor Peter was no doubt freshening up for his anticipated rendezvous with me."

"We've only delayed him a few hours," he reminded. "So, soon as we get checked into the Zilver Inn, we better start working."

"Exactly," she said. "I'll start contacting my informants tonight. Do you want to come along or—"

"No, I'm going to try a direct approach on Dr. Mayerling."

"Tonight?"

"Yep, in the dark."

"This may sound superstitious, but Mayerling seems like the sort of fellow best approached by daylight, bright sunny daylight."

"By the time we get our next sunlight hereabouts, Jennie, Peter Starr McMillion will be in town."

The auburn-haired reporter nodded at the curtained window. "Dunkelstein doesn't have a single telephone yet, you know."

"I do, which is why I'll arrange for a carriage to take me out there. Blackwood Castle is only about fifteen miles out of town."

Finished with the rose, she slipped both hands under the robe. "I bet at night, traveling through the Blackwood Forest," she said, "it'll seem a heck of a lot longer."

Harry, alone and whistling softly, took a walk through the lanes and byways of Dunkelstein. The rain had subsided into a gently falling mist.

A hired carriage would call for him at nine at the Zilver Inn. The innkeeper had arranged for the transportation, insisting that Harry must pay double the usual fee because the destination was Blackwood Castle and warning him the driver must leave the vicinity of the castle well before midnight struck.

Jennie had taken off from the inn a few minutes ahead of Harry, bound for a meeting with the occult expert who was one of her sources of information.

She'd looked very pretty in her rain cape.

"Not as pretty as Alicia, though," Harry felt obliged to remind himself.

He whistled a slower tune, pausing to look into a toymaker's dimly lit shop window. Rag dolls were sprawled in a heap, at least a dozen of them, floppy arms and legs tangled and twined. A long parade of soldiers stood frozen in front of the tumble of fat dolls. Dangling down from above was a blond ballerina puppet.

Harry moved on.

From a pastry shop cafe spilled yellow light, loud conversations and the strong scent of cinnamon.

". . . no, no, that is not the way it goes, Max," someone was arguing inside.

"I am right, Moritz."

"No, no, Max. The man takes the sheepdog up to the front door and . . ."

Harry turned a corner to find himself walking down a steep incline. There had been a fire on this street recently; the black smell of it was still hanging in the damp air. The two shops on his right were gutted, a jumble of broken wine bottles could be seen in among the charred and fallen timbers of one. It was impossible to tell what sort of business had been carried on in the other shop.

Just beyond the ruined stores was a narrow twist of alley. Huddled in it, on her knees, was a dark-haired young woman in a dark cloak.

Standing over her was a wide-shouldered young man in a tattered peacoat. He had a butcher knife in his raised right hand.

". . . please . . . don't," the fallen girl pleaded in a faint voice.

"I don't think you'd better touch her," said Harry.

The youth spun, facing Harry. His face was soft and moonlight white, his eyes small and red-rimmed. "Mind your own damn business, outlander."

Saying nothing, Harry suddenly kicked the young man in the knee. "You ought," he suggested, kicking him in his other knee, "to be cordial to tourists, lad. They're good for the local economy."

The young man was howling in pain, doubled over, trying to rub at his knees.

Harry next dealt a paralyzing blow to the youth's knife arm, and the blade clattered to the slick cobblestones.

"Swine!" Turning, he went hobbling off, picking up speed the farther downhill he got.

"People keep calling me that," murmured Harry, watching the departure.

"Thank you," said the dark-haired young woman. She was standing now, cloak wrapped tight around her. She was tall, nearly as tall as Harry, and quite attractive. "I should be all right now."

"How far are you from home?"

"Only a mile or so," she answered. "I am certain I shan't have—"

"Still and all," he told her, "I'd better see you home."

"Very well," she said, smiling faintly. "That would be most kind of you."

She put her hand on his proffered arm. He could feel the coldness of her touch through his coat sleeve.

Chapter 11

Harry dropped more sticks into the small fireplace. The fire crackled and sputtered but still didn't seem to produce much heat.

"You've been most kind," said the dark-haired young woman, who'd introduced herself as Naida Strand. She sat, dark cloak still wrapped around her, in a carved wooden chair close to the heatless fireplace.

Carved serpents chased frightened hares up the thick legs of the chair.

"You're certain," inquired Harry, "you don't know the gent who attacked you?"

"I haven't any notion who the man was, no." She held both pale hands out to the thin fire.

They were in the parlor of her cottage, a stunted gray-stone and red-tile place on the edge of town. The walls were a dead white color, slanting oddly inward, as though the room had been designed by someone with a faulty sense of perspective. The only light, besides the feeble fire, came from a hurricane lamp on the small wooden table beside Naida.

"I wouldn't have figured Dunkelstein," said Harry, "for a town with many footpads and robbers roaming its streets of an evening."

"My stay here has been peaceful and untroubled
. . . until tonight." She stood up, slowly and gracefully. "Might I offer you a cup of tea before you take
your leave?"

Harry tugged his watch from his watch pocket.
"Sure, if you're up to fixing it."

"I am." She moved silently out of the chill room.

Hands in trouser pockets, Harry took a slow stroll
around the grim parlor.

There were only two small windows, both high up
and made of jigsaw chunks of thick stained glass.
Tree branches scratched at them. A lame claw-footed
table stood beneath one window, its surface covered
with a varied collection of objects—a dumpy pewter
vase filled with dusty straw flowers, three small
glass globes housing snow scenes within, a crystal
egg. One of the globes, which Harry lifted and up-
ended, had a ruined castle inside. The make-believe
snow swirled around its broken battlements.

All along one shadowy wall ran a series of dark
wood shelves. Fat old leather-bound books mingled
with small stuffed birds, polished stone lizards and
toads and tiny little people made of blown glass. The
gilded titles of most of the books were blurred, not
legible. Selecting a book at random, Harry opened it.
The pages were musty and foxed. Once, long ago,
someone had pressed a yellow rose between them. It
was brittle and nearly black, with the stem twisted
like the tail of a lizard. The text was in Latin.

"Do you read Latin?" asked Naida behind him.

"I was able to while I was in high school," he replied, closing the book and returning it to its place.
"The knack's long since deserted me."

She was wearing a full-length gown of dark velvet,
held in at the waist with a thin cord of gold. A ruby

pendant hung around her neck on a golden chain. "You're an American, I assume." She set the copper tray she was carrying on the table beside her chair and poured two cups of tea from the plump purple teapot.

"Yes, from New York." He accepted the cup of tea she handed him.

"An exciting city, I hear. Do you prefer it, say, to London or Paris?"

Harry sipped his tea, which was strong bitter stuff. "You didn't include Zevenburg on your list."

A very thin smile touched her face. "It is a charming city, yet I don't believe it compares with Paris or Vienna," she replied. "Although I did pick up this lovely brooch in Zevenburg." She lifted the chain and the lamplight flashed in the deep red stone. "It's quite fascinating, don't you think?"

Harry had to be interested in jewels professionally, but he wasn't much fascinated by them otherwise. "It's—" Yet this ruby, ticking slowly back and forth on the glittering chain, was fascinating.

It pulsed, like a small beating heart, and he couldn't keep from watching it.

Seeing, in fact, nothing else.

The walls and the floor were growing dim, dimmer, fading away, swallowed by deep shadows.

The ruby was there.

And Naida's eyes.

Then there was nothing but shadows.

Peter Starr McMillion said, "Look on the bright side, Tubbs."

His stocky valet was bent under the weight of the steamer trunk he was lugging across the misty courtyard of the Zilver Inn. "There hain't no bloody bright side to this 'ere fiasco, guv," he growled.

Swinging his small valise in his gloved hand, the tall handsome McMillion said, "We had a pleasant and invigorating climb up the mountainside once we made our way out of our derailed private rail car, Tubbs old man," he pointed out. "Then a brisk and healthful hike over the pastoral highways and byways of this delightful—"

"Muddy is what it were."

"One can never have enough exercise." The journalist pushed open the doors of the inn. "Don't forget, Tubbs, we rode the final fourteen miles."

"In a bloomin' wagon full of goats. Foul beggars, they was." Tubbs dumped the trunk down on a bright throw rug. "An' me carryin' this blinkin' wardrobe trunk on me poor frail back till me beantosser fair to fell off."

"I'm on a mission," McMillion said as he approached the deserted desk. "I need my disguises."

" 'Ow the bloomin' 'ell are yer goin' ter hutilize a complete wog disguise in this 'ere benighted 'ole? These wooden 'eads don't know a burnoose from a bullock's tallywag." Tugging a polka-dot handkerchief out from a lumpy pocket of his mud-spattered greatcoat, he wiped at his forehead. "Or 'ow about your southern darky costume, guv? That'd merely scare these Krauts out of—"

"One never knows which disguise will be called for. Hence, Tubbs, we must bring them all." He rapped the hardwood desktop with his fist.

"The deep-sea diver outfit, that's another what weighs a bloody ton," grumbled Tubbs as he sat on the muddy trunk he'd been hefting. "Complete with 'elmet. You'd think we was halways on the bloomin' verge of hattendin' a blinkin' fancy dress ball. Hit's enough ter give a man a pain in 'is ruddy gravy-maker."

No one emerged from the tiny office behind the registration desk to attend to the new guests. "I say," McMillion called in a polite, but louder, voice, "might one be shown to one's room?"

"Might one get a boil on one's fundament waitin'." Tubbs dug a hand under his greatcoat to scratch at his armpit. "I'll tell yer once hagain to 'oom we owe this fine feathered predicament, guv. That skinny freckled grummett, is 'oo. Never did like 'er, special after that time in Valparaiso when—"

"I'll thank you, Tubbs, not to refer to Miss Barr as a grummett. Whatever that might be."

Tubbs spit into his fist. "Makes a bloomin' king's ransom for merely scribblin' words on paper, yet don't know that a grummett is a bellydingle, a cunnikin, a—"

"Yes, I suspected as much." Deftly, he reached behind the registration desk and brought up the register. Opening it to the page for that day, he scanned the names of the guests. "Ah, speak of the devil, as it were. Miss Barr is registered here at this selfsame inn."

" 'Ooray fer that news. Might be you an' me can dress up like a wog an' a red Indian an' take 'er dancin' in the rain."

"Jove, Harry Challenge is here as well."

"Hin the same bloomin' room as the quiff, I'll wager."

"Now then, Tubbs, no more of that," warned the renowned journalist. "Miss Barr is certainly not that sort of young woman."

"Just 'cause you been unhable to get inter 'er

knickers, guv, don't mean this 'Arry is so dumb," observed his valet. "Them Hamericans is quick as weasels. The ol' twanger can slip in afore—"

"Enough," cautioned McMillion again. "Ah, but here comes our boniface now."

The heavyset, white-haired innkeeper had come puffing out of the kitchen, face flushed, wearing a white apron over his dark suit. "Forgive me, sirs," he apologized as he ducked behind the desk. "I didn't realize you were waiting out here. You should've rung the little silver bell there."

"We didn't 'ave the strength, guv," said Tubbs, arising wearily from the trunk.

"Eh?"

"Merely a jest," explained McMillion. "I am Peter Starr McMillion. I have a reservation for myself·and my man."

"Of course, of course." He turned the register toward him. "We are honored, sir."

Tubbs was scowling at the knickknack shelves on the wall. "I don't himagine they 'as one decent bordello in this 'ole bloomin' town," he observed.

Chapter 12

In the article she'd written about him for *Scribner's* magazine two years ago, Jennie had described Professor Wilhelm Staub, then the head of the history department at prestigious Zevenburg University, as being leonine in appearance. Here in his comfortable, tidy study, the word still struck her as apt.

Staub, retired now, was a large, broad-shouldered man with long straw-colored hair. Although he had given up tobacco, he still liked to chew on a disreputable pipe. He wore rimless spectacles low on his wide, flat nose and looked over them as often as through them.

The professor was seated behind his large wooden desk, open books and a sheaf of papers arranged neatly in front of him. He had a half-full beer mug resting on a wooden coaster near his right elbow. "I've learned a good deal more since last I wrote to you."

Jennie, sitting in a large leather armchair near his desk, had been staring into the blazing fire in the deep stone fireplace. "Beg pardon?"

"Thinking of something else, little Jennie?"

"Someone else," she said.

"You did not come alone to Dunkelstein?"

"I intended to, but I ran into—well, a friend of mine on the train."

"A good friend, judging by the tone of your voice." He took a sip of his beer.

"I have mixed feelings about that," she said. "I'll tell you about him, and the unusual things that happened on our trip here, in a while. First tell me what you've learned, Willie."

Staub picked up the handwritten pages. "Three hundred years ago," he began, "in the wild mountain region of the country of Lusitania, there flourished a gentleman named Karl Mayerling. He was a scientist of sorts who—"

"Any relation to our Dr. Mayerling?"

"It is the same man."

Jennie suddenly sat up straight. "How the heck can he have stayed alive all these—"

"Mayerling engaged in very dangerous scientific and magical researches," the professor said, tapping the manuscript with the bowl of his pipe.

Jennie said, "You're trying to tell me, Willie, that he found the secret of immortality?"

"Not yet, no, but he continues to work on it. This rejuvenation sanitarium has been set up mainly to provide him with disciples who'll supply financing for his researches."

"Wait now," the reporter said. "If Mayerling didn't find out how to become immortal through science and magic, how'd he manage to hang around so long beyond his alloted three score and ten?"

"By becoming a vampire," the professor answered.

The carriage creaked and groaned as it rolled along the forest road. The window on the righthand side was broken, and misty night air drifted in through the jagged opening. The tall dark trees were tangled in mist, too.

Harry sat gazing out the empty window, hands folded in his lap. Gradually, as the carriage rattled along, he commenced shivering some.

There was something he ought to be doing, but he couldn't quite remember what it was.

"Let's see now," he said to himself, "I'd better review the facts of the case."

What case?

That question presented a problem.

He was going somewhere, that much was obvious.

"Blackwood Castle," he recalled.

He'd arranged to have a carriage call for him at the Zilver Inn at nine, to take him out to the castle in the Blackwood Forest.

"Simple enough."

Except he had absolutely no recollection of having stepped into his carriage.

He hadn't even, he was nearly sure, gone back to the inn after . . .

After what?

"I went for a walk."

Right, a walk. The toymaker's, the cafe, the burnt-out wine shop. But after that . . .

"There's a gap," he realized, taking out his gold watch.

The hour was ten-thirty.

"The last time I checked the time it was . . ."

He couldn't remember that.

The carriage came to a dead stop.

Harry looked out.

There didn't seem to be anything about but trees.

"This might be," it occurred to him, "a hell of an appropriate time to have a chat with my driver."

He located the door handle after a while. When he opened the door and looked down, he couldn't see the ground, only the thick gray mist.

After hesitating a moment, Harry stepped into the night.

The road wasn't exactly where he anticipated, and he stumbled, went down on one knee.

Something scurried away into the crosshatch of dark trees and branches.

He got to his feet and, by bracing one hand on the side of the chill, damp carriage, made his way around to the front.

There were two black horses in the traces, both standing silent and patient.

But there was no driver.

"Funny," remarked Harry as he glanced around.

He noticed a faint glow a hundred yards or so up the misty night road.

"Must be the damn driver."

Harry started walking.

The light was a lantern.

A woman in a gray cloak was holding it. Not a young woman, someone in her late fifties.

He walked another dozen feet before he recognized her.

It was his mother.

Harry was very anxious to talk to her, because up to now he'd been under the impression she'd been dead for over six years.

Chapter 13

Twirling his gold-headed cane like a baton, the Great Lorenzo was walking briskly along the Nussdorferstrasse. He had roughly forty-five minutes, the time between his first and second shows, to accomplish what he had in mind.

This section of the city was modest yet well-kept. The streetlamps were still of the gas variety and they glowed hazily in the night mist. Far up the block a delivery wagon was being pulled by a woebegone gray mare. Just around the corner, unseen, two stray cats were either courting or squabbling.

"Ah, my sought-after goal." The portly magician bounded up the steps of the narrow three-story boardinghouse.

Spying no bellpull, he rapped on the glass panel of the front door with his cane.

In the poorly lit corridor he saw a door open. A thin, tall man in a faded silk smoking jacket emerged and came hobbling to the door.

"We have no rooms," he called through the glass. "Good night, go away."

"I am not in need of lodging, my friend," boomed the magician. "I am Herr Doctor Korkzieher, the noted attorney, come to see you about your legacy."

"Eh?" The man's sharp nose pressed against the glass. "Is there money?"

"Immense quantities."

The door swung open. "From where?" inquired the landlord.

"You do, or rather did, have a great uncle named Gustav Dirks?"

"No, I never heard— Ah, but you must mean dear Uncle Gus? Is he the one who—"

"We have much to discuss, Herr Kummer." The Great Lorenzo took hold of his arm, urged him along the hallway to his open door. "We can talk in your suite. Are you alone this evening?"

"Yes, Herr Korkzieher. My wife is visiting with her—"

"Jolly. Then we needn't bother her with all the financial details, eh?"

"No, Elana has no head for figures. How much did my poor uncle leave me to—"

"They haven't finished counting the money yet," explained the magician as he shooed Kummer across his own threshold.

"So much then?"

"Your dear departed uncle was an eccentric man, as you well know."

"Oh . . . yes, yes. We often remarked of it in the family."

"Precisely. He had wads of money hidden here, bundles of bank notes stashed there. A real mare's nest and a great challenge to my clerks."

"I can well understand that."

The parlor was cluttered. Ponderous furniture, chairs, tables, sofas, stood everywhere. There were bell glasses covering plaster statues, vases of artificial flowers, books and bookends, all crowding on tabletops. Hassocks and stuffed pillows filled the floor space on the thick flowered carpet between the heavier pieces of furniture.

"Before we get down to business," said the Great Lorenzo, "I'd very much appreciate your looking at this gold medallion."

"My uncle left this to me as well?" Kummer squinted at the coin-size medallion that was rotating between the magician's forefinger and middle finger.

"We're not certain. What I'd like you to do, sir, is look at it. Carefully . . . that's right . . . look at it . . . look while I gently rotate it in my supple fingers . . . look at it . . . forget everything . . . think of sleep . . . sleep and rest . . . very good . . . Now sit yourself down on the godawful purple armchair . . . Fine . . ."

The hypnotized landlord sank into the fat chair.

Nudging over a tufted hassock with his knee, the magician sat facing him. "Some months ago you rented rooms here to one Wolfgang Spangler."

"I'm not supposed to talk about that."

"Ah, yet you will. That's the very reason I've bothered to put you in this classy trance, my boy," the Great Lorenzo explained. "Now then. Tell me all about Spangler."

"He only stayed a week."

"And then?"

"They took him away."

"Who performed that little service?"

"I was paid not to tell. To deny he was ever here."

"You'll tell me, though."

"They didn't think I knew who they were really working for," droned Kummer. "Think I'm a fool. But I recognized one of them. I'd seen him once when

Mama and I were vacationing in the Blackwood Forest. He pretended to be the head man when they came here, but I knew he was the minion of . . ."

"Continue."

"I shouldn't give his name. He's a very powerful man. He could order harm done to me."

"You will tell me. That's the splendid thing about hypnosis. You'll give me the name of the man you suspect is behind all this."

"Dark Otto."

"Baron Otto Van Horn?"

"The same. He will kill me."

"Highly unlikely," the magician assured him. "Where did Dark Otto's men take Spangler?"

"That I don't know."

The Great Lorenzo drummed his fingers on his knee. "What were your instructions?"

"Should anyone come looking for Spangler, I was to say he'd never been here," answered the entranced landlord. "Whatever mail came for him I was to hand over to them."

"Where?"

"I took it and left it at the Pavilion of Automatons, at our Exposition."

"Dark Otto," muttered the Great Lorenzo, standing. "Most interesting. You've been a joy to converse with, Herr Kummer, even though you're not an especially admirable fellow." He made his way around the furniture to the door. "You'll fall completely asleep now, then awaken in one hour with no memory of my little visit at all. Oh, but you'll have a desire to buy the most expensive seat you can get for an early performance of the Great Lorenzo's magic show. You won't feel right until you've seen that spectacular entertainment at least twice. And you'll advise all your cronies to do likewise." He bowed. "Good evening, sir."

Jennie had stood up. "I have to get back to the inn," she told Professor Staub, "right away."

"What's wrong?" He too rose.

"If what you say about Dr. Mayerling is true, then—"

"It's true, the fellow is a vampire." He thumped the papers upon his desk. "There can be no doubt. But why—"

"My friend, Harry Challenge— He's a private investigator from New York who—" She gave an impatient shake of her head. "Oh, there isn't time to go into the darn details. Harry's planning to drive out to Blackwood Castle tonight to confront the doctor. He doesn't know Mayerling's a vampire and—"

"Yes, you'd best warn him to stay clear of that place by night," agreed the professor, anticipating what she was going to say.

The clock on the mantel chimed for the quarter hour.

"I've only got fifteen minutes to catch him." Jennie hurried to the door.

"Bring the young man back later, if you can." Staub opened the door for her. "We should talk, all of us."

Stepping out into the misty night, Jennie called back, "I will, yes. Goodbye for now, Willie."

She walked rapidly, in the long-striding tomboy way she used when she was anxious and in a hurry. The rain had a cold, gritty feel on her face.

Heading back for the Zilver Inn, she thought she was retracing the route she'd used going to the professor's house. Somewhere, though, she took a wrong turning.

Jennie found herself skirting a tiny park area. It had a rusted wrought-iron fence enclosing its weedy, overgrown half a square block of grounds. The nearest gate was sprung, hanging at an odd angle.

Stopping still, Jennie glanced around and sought to get her bearings. It was very difficult, with the mist closed in and the buildings blurred, to spot anything like a familiar landmark.

The high grass in the abandoned park was rustling, swaying as though something was moving through it close to the ground.

Jennie started walking back the way she'd come.

The rustling kept up. Whatever it was in the grass was keeping pace with her.

She crossed the street.

All the houses and shops huddled along this unknown street seemed dead. There was no sound, no light.

Someone was waiting for her.

Up ahead, leaning against a lamppost. A small man in a gray suit, rubbing his hands nervously together.

She recognized him when she was fifty yards off. "But that can't be," she whispered to herself.

It was the man she'd killed on the train. Gruber.

Chapter 14

She called to Harry across the foggy night and the voice was absolutely right. The woman standing there in the night woods, no doubt about it, was his mother.

"Come along now, son, there's a good deal we have to talk about." Lowering the lantern to her side, the gray-haired woman turned away and began walking deeper into the forest.

Harry was still a distance from her. "Wait, Mom," he said. "Give me a chance to catch up."

She moved swiftly, almost floating, away from him. The light bobbed and danced between the trees.

"I thought you were dead," Harry called as he followed her. "I'm glad to see you're not. This way . . . when you died I was out in Chicago on that swindling case. I . . . you know, by the time I got back home you were gone. There were things I'd intended to say . . ."

He couldn't get any nearer to her. She was up ahead, walking fast.

When he was a kid, that would happen. His mother'd be thinking of something, get to walking fast. Harry'd be looking into shop windows or watching the street life. All at once they'd both realize what had happened. She'd stand there and wait; he'd go running to catch up.

Yes, and she was doing that now. Up ahead. His mother had stopped, waiting, beckoning him to hurry to her.

"The thing is . . ." He slowed, struggling to catch an idea that was trying to form.

"Harry, please, come along," she urged.

"The thing is," he said aloud, "you're dead and gone."

Yes, he came home from Chicago in time for the funeral. He'd seen her in her coffin.

Harry took a deep breath, shaking his head. His fists were clenching and he was shivering. He made himself stop walking.

They were only a few feet apart now, Harry and his mother.

"Come here, Harry darling." The lantern was resting on the mossy ground, her arms were open to him.

"You're dead," he told her. "This has to be . . . an illusion . . . a hallucination . . ."

"Harry, oh, don't say that. You'll spoil everything."

"Mayerling . . . This has to be Dr. Mayerling," he said. "He had that damn Strand woman . . . slip me something . . . do something." He was sweating, breathing hard. It was a fight not to go closer to his mother.

"Harry . . ."

She began to fade, slowly shimmering away to nothing. Even the lantern vanished, giving way to darkness.

The ground changed, too.

Harry looked down to find he was standing at the

very edge of a pit. Hands shaking some, he lit a match.

The pit was some sort of animal trap. The bottom of it, six feet below, was lined with sharp-pointed sticks, all pointing up at Harry out of the grave-smelling earth.

Carefully, he took a step back and then another. He turned, began making his way to the road.

He thought he heard his mother call after him once, faint and far away.

He kept walking away from there.

Gruber said, "Good evening, Fräulein Barr." His voice was dry, rasping.

Jennie thrust her hand into her shoulder bag. "I still have the same gun," she warned, tugging it out into the open. "I killed you once, I'll do it again."

His walk was a bit off. He lurched, swayed, as he came for her. "That won't, I fear, work this time," Gruber informed her. "I would like you, please, to come along with—"

"Like heck!" She fired two silver bullets into his chest.

They made dull clanking sounds.

This wasn't Gruber at all. This was some kind of simulacrum, one of those clockwork figures Harry'd told her about.

Then the thing to do was disable it.

Aiming at the approaching automaton's head, she prepared to shoot again.

Something hit her in the legs, hard, from behind. Jennie stumbled, caught a glimpse of a large black dog. It must be the thing that was in the park.

She swung the gun up.

But Gruber was right there. He swung his heavy
fist.

The blow hit her in the temple. Her teeth rattled.
She let go, not meaning to, of her gun.

The next two blows were harder.

She fell, but never had the sensation of hitting the
damp cobblestones. Instead, she was swallowed up by
mist.

"Hit makes yer ponder," observed Tubbs as he
tested the mattress on Jennie's spoolbed with his
backside. "With locks so easy ter pick hin this 'ere
hinn, why, nobody's valuables is—"

"Do try to be less boisterous, old fellow," cautioned McMillion. He had the lady reporter's suitcase open on the floor and was kneeling beside it.
"We don't want the innkeeper—"

"Gor, 'e's deaf as a post." He settled on the bed,
short legs dangling, to watch his employer search
through Jennie's belongings. " 'Ow do yer feel 'andlin' 'er underwear? Pal o' mine in Lime'ouse, ever'
time 'e so much as squinted hat a pair of knickers,
why, 'is fiddlestick grew to a henormous—"

"Hush," advised the journalist. "We don't have
that much time before Miss Barr may return from
her visit to—"

"She's more 'n likely carousin' in some low dive,
hif they 'as such a thing in this rinkydink town, with
'Andsome 'Arry the detective."

"No, Tubbs, the innkeeper assured me they'd gone
off separately. Miss Barr, furthermore, had inquired
as how best to reach Wissenschaftstrasse."

"The innkeeper hain't the smartest bloke on this
green earth, guv. 'E wouldn't even know where 'is
rumpsplitter were hif it weren't attached to—"

"Ah, this is quite interesting." He was holding an envelope in his gloved hand. "Written to Miss Barr from a Professor Staub of 72 Wissenschaftstrasse, this town." Nodding to himself, he extracted the letter from the envelope.

Tubbs left the bed to prowl the white-walled room. " 'Ow about this now?" he said, picking up a small framed photograph from atop the heavy chest of drawers. "Didn't I tell yer 'Arry was dippin' the ol' plowshare inter—"

"Quiet." McMillion was reading through the professor's letter, frowning. "Things are much more serious than I was aware."

"Is the prof rollin' in the 'ay with Jennie as well?"

McMillion's frown deepened. "This has to do with Dr. Mayerling."

"The very bloke you've come all this bloomin' way to get a yarn on?"

"The same, yes." He'd refolded the letter, was rubbing it across his handsome chin. "According to this Professor Staub, the doctor is involved in much more than fleecing foolish British millionaires. The original focus of my article must be severely modified, I'm afraid."

"What's the doc up ter?"

"Black magic and sorcery."

Tubbs chortled. "Ar, there hain't no such thing. You can't really, guv, believe—"

"Don't scoff, Tubbs," warned McMillion. "In my travels around this giddy globe, old man, I've encountered a good many strange things. No, I most certainly wouldn't rule out the possibility that Dr. Mayerling is indeed a sorcerer of sorts."

Shrugging, the valet held up the photo he'd discovered. "Suppose yer take a gander hat this," he sug-

gested. "Hindicates the wench his far gone on friend
'Arry." It was a small studio portrait, sepia-toned, of
a younger Harry Challenge. He was standing in
front of a pastoral painted backdrop, his elbow resting on a marble pedestal.

"Not inscribed, I notice," said McMillion, returning his attention to the contents of the young woman's suitcase. "In fact, one imagines the Challenge
International Detective Agency, being a vulgar and
aggressive organization, hands such photographs
out as advertisements."

"Be 'at as it may," said the smirking Tubbs, passing the framed photograph under his mangled nose,
"this smells orful sweet, guv. I'd say she keeps it
close to 'er much of the time. Therefore, yer chances
of—"

"Allow me to conclude this search. Time is running out."

"What do we do arfter this bit of snoopin'?"

"Ah, here's a list of those in Dunkelstein Jennie
intends to call upon. Jolly." He gazed at the new-
found list for a few seconds. "There, got it memo-
rized. What were you asking, old fellow?"

"I was curious, guv, has to what fun-filled hactivity
we'd be engagin' in once we left this bloomin' 'ole.
That is, when yer through diggin' inter m'lady's underwear."

"I have a hunch we'd be wise to follow in Miss
Barr's footsteps this evening," replied McMillion.
"Yes, one imagines that might well lead to some-
thing of interest."

Chapter 15

A rooster crowed as Harry came trudging toward the outskirts of Dunkelstein. Yawning, Harry brushed at the sawdust that was still clinging to his trousers.

He'd gotten a ride to within a mile of town in the back of a woodcutter's cart.

The day was about to commence; the last of the night was fading away. The grass along the side of the road was thick with dew. Birds were twittering.

And Harry, although he had recovered from whatever potion or spell Naida Strand had used on him, was a shade confused.

"They keep trying to kill me," he reflected, passing the first of the thatched cottages at the edge of town. "With a demented automaton, then with a wolfman." He spit at the road. "And, hell, I don't even completely believe in werewolves."

Then last night they'd set up that whole business with the dark-haired Naida. Turned him near stupefied, tried to lure him into toppling down into that damn pit full of sharp stakes.

"Would've looked like an accident. Tourist, not too bright to begin with, gets lost in woods and falls in animal trap."

Why was Mayerling going to all this trouble? Just to keep him from talking to Jonah Mariott?

"They didn't even know I was on the case when they turned that mechanical man loose on me," he reminded himself again.

He was anxious to talk to Jennie, to find out what she'd learned from Professor Staub and her other contacts in town. Harry had decided he had to be better informed before he went up against Dr. Mayerling.

A bread wagon rolled by, trailing the pleasant scent of fresh-baked bread.

Harry knew there was no sense going back to Naida's cottage. He didn't figure she'd still be residing there.

"Damn, if that fake attack on her had been staged on Broadway, I never would've fallen for it."

Over here in the Old World, though, he'd let his guard down, acted as gullible as a hick tourist.

A plump little black pup came barking at Harry when he entered the early morning courtyard of the Zilver Inn.

"Hush, hush, Otto," ordered the stableboy in a loud whisper.

"Another Dark Otto, huh?" Harry said to the animal.

Tail wagging, the black pup circled Harry once before running into the stable to attack a pile of straw.

The desk area was deserted. A lazy horsefly was walking over the counter top.

Harry bounded up the stairs, hurried along the hall and knocked lightly on the door of Jennie's room.

His knock caused the unlocked door to swing slowly inward.

Harry was just taking in the fact that no one was in the room and that Jennie's bed hadn't been slept in when a pair of powerful arms grabbed him from behind.

"Bloody barbarian," grumbled Tubbs. He was sitting on a low stone wall, legs dangling, rubbing at the new welt on his forehead.

"That'll be quite enough, old fellow," instructed McMillion.

He and Harry were walking slowly around the little flagstone square near the inn. Early morning sunlight was starting to brighten the area, making the water in the circular fountain glitter.

"Toss a hinnocent workin' stiff inter a bloomin' wall," said the aggrieved valet, scowling at Harry. "When hall I was doin' were hinvitin' 'im to a little rendezvous with me—"

"Hush."

Harry, hands in his trouser pockets, said, "Where's Jennie?"

"That's just it, old man. I don't know, don't have the faintest idea."

"She didn't come back to the inn last night?"

McMillion shook his head. "One realizes the habits of American journalists are somewhat more relaxed than those of us in England who—"

"She didn't spend the night with anybody," Harry told him.

"Exactly the point I'm making, Challenge," said the handsome journalist. "You are rather keen on her, though, aren't you?"

"Look, I didn't agree to this meeting just to play

advice-to-the-lovelorn with you, McMillion." Halting, he took hold of the man's arm. "I want to find Jennie. So you—"

" 'Ere now! Don't go man'andlin' the guv," warned Tubbs from his perch, "else I'll climb down an'—"

"I don't," said Harry, turning briefly to stare at him, "want to hear one more single goddamn word from you."

"Gor." Tubbs closed his mouth tight.

"There's no need for any internecine fighting, old man. I'm very concerned over Jennie, too, Challenge. If you'll but hear me out, I—"

"Get on with it then."

"She left the Zilver Inn last evening shortly after eight," said McMillion, "to call on a Professor Staub."

"That I already know."

"To be sure, yet I wager you don't know that the professor was the only one she called on."

"How do you know that?"

"I happen, by the merest chance, to have had access to a list of her intended interviewees," he explained, watching the dolphin spray water into the pool of the fountain. "She left Staub's residence at approximately nine. Nothing is known of her activities thereafter, I'm afraid."

"You've talked to Staub?"

"I have," replied McMillion, coughing into his gloved fist. "He was, I must admit, deuced difficult. Gave me, don't you know, only the curtest of answers. He did imply, however, that he would be much more open with you, Challenge, which is one of the reasons I've sought you out."

"And what the hell do you get out of all this?"

"Jove, man, I'm concerned about Jennie." He

drew himself up, throwing his broad shoulders back. "I also have a story to do, concerning the activities of this Dr. Mayerling chap."

Harry released his arm. "You talked to the others on the list."

"There were three. I sought out each and, although it involved rousing them out of slumber in two cases, questioned them thoroughly," said Mc-Million. "None saw Jennie Barr last evening."

"Unless one of them is lying."

"They wasn't," contributed Tubbs. "When I sits in on the hinterviews, you gets very little lyin'."

Harry said, "I'll go see Professor Staub right now, then see if I can pick up Jennie's trail."

"No doubt we'll find Dr. Mayerling's hand in this affair."

"Probably," said Harry. "But before I head out for Blackwood Castle, I want to talk to Staub."

Smiling, McMillion said, "Splendid, Challenge. Together we ought to be able to—"

"I don't intend to work with you on this, McMillion."

"But, I say, that's damned unsporting. After one's confided one's innermost—"

"And if you send that lunkhead after me again—" Harry jerked a thumb in Tubbs's direction. "I'll do more than just bounce him off the wall."

He went striding off across the flagstones of the square.

"You believe all this?"

"Don't you?"

Harry drank some of the coffee in the mug the leonine Professor Staub had provided. "Guess I have to."

Staub was behind his massive desk, notes and manuscript pages spread out before him. "There can be little doubt that Dr. Mayerling is a vampire," he said.

"And you got Jennie interested in doing a story about him?"

"She is a very capable young woman, as you well know, Herr Challenge." He shook his head. "Many times before she has faced danger."

"Sure, but this is a mite different from tribal wars and tenement fires," Harry said from the leather armchair. "There's sorcery and—"

"Evil. You shy at the word."

"Evil then." Putting his cup on a marble-top table, Harry rose. "What do we do now?"

The professor steepled his fingers. "There are two possibilities we have to face, neither one pleasant."

"Yeah, either Jennie's dead or she's a prisoner of Mayerling." He went to the windows, stared unseeing at the morning street.

"I'm inclined to think the latter," Staub said. "Alive she has some value to him as a hostage, someone he can use to pressure you and his other enemies."

"I tried to get out there last night to see him, but—"

"Blackwood Castle is a dangerous place after sunset," said the professor. "Even in the brightest daylight it—"

"He's got Jennie and he'll want to bargain. I'm going to talk to him."

"It might be best to—"

"I'm way beyond doing the wisest thing," Harry told him. "I don't want to do some damn fool thing that'll jeopardize her, but I'm going to see Mayerling today."

From a desk drawer Professor Staub took a silver religious medal. Saying nothing, he handed it to Harry.

Chapter 16

The horse Harry rented from the livery stable at the edge of town was an amiable roan mare. She carried him that morning at a steady gallop through the Blackwood Forest.

By day the woodlands weren't particularly ominous. Sunlight came slanting down through the high branches, birds sang, squirrels scurried up and down the broad trunks.

Although he was on the lookout for the spot where his carriage had stopped last evening, he wasn't able to find it. It was the same road, yet not all of it was familiar. He had a momentary uneasiness, wondering if he'd see his mother again, the image of her beckoning him from beside the roadway. But that passed.

When Harry was roughly a mile from his destination, he began to notice the silence. No birds called, no animals moved in the brush. The sun didn't feel as warm as it had.

"Imagination," he told himself.

He rode his mount around a bend in the forest road, and there was the castle.

It rose up from a clearing a hundred yards ahead, an immense brooding structure of dark gray stone

and dark tile. There were turrets, towers, battlements. A high stone wall surrounded the three acres
covered by the castle and its grounds.

And riding out through the open oaken doors of
the courtyard came a neatly dressed young man on a
bicycle.

"Whoa," Harry suggested to his mare, reining up.

A trio of dark broad-winged birds took flight from
the north tower, cawing loudly as they circled higher
and higher into the thin blue of the morning.

"Would it be Mr. Challenge?" inquired the young
man when his bicycle was opposite Harry. He was
clad in a Norfolk suit of grayish prickly material,
had a straw hat on his head, and wore gold-rimmed
spectacles. He stopped his black bicycle, smiled up at
Harry. "I am Dr. Mistley."

"Pleased to meet you." Harry swung down out of
the saddle. "No need to give you my card, Doctor,
since you already know who I am."

"I practiced medicine in Manhattan for nearly two
years," said the smiling doctor. "I'm not as young as
I look. At any rate, I heard a good deal about you in
those days, and you were pointed out to me on more
than one occasion."

Nodding toward the huge gray castle, Harry asked,
"You work with Mayerling?"

Mistley removed his spectacles, polished the lenses
carefully with his white pocket handkerchief. When
he took off the glasses, his pale blue eyes began to
water. "He's doing remarkable work here," he answered. "I'm quite proud to be associated with him."

"I've come to see him."

Replacing the spectacles and grinning, Dr. Mistley
said, "You're much too early for that, I'm afraid. Dr.
Mayerling is a late riser."

Harry was looking at the castle. "Indeed?"

Vampires were supposed to sleep by day. Maybe Professor Staub was absolutely right about Mayerling.

"I might be able to arrange an interview with Dr. Mayerling late this afternoon."

"Little after sundown maybe?"

"About then, yes," said Mistley. "However, I'm familiar with the entire functioning of our sanitarium and—"

"You have a patient named Jonah Mariott?"

"Of course. A fellow American and an amiable gentleman. He and I have had many an enjoyable evening of whist since his—"

"Could I talk with Mariott?"

"Now, do you mean? Today?"

"Soon as possible."

"You're not related," said the young doctor.

"I'm working for his niece and nephew, both of whom are very concerned about—"

"He's in excellent condition, both physically and mentally, Mr. Challenge. I can assure you that Dr. Mayerling's treatments have worked veritable mirac—"

"Not that I doubt your word, Doctor," cut in Harry. "Until I talk to him direct, though, I won't be satisfied."

"That's only natural, yes," admitted Dr. Mistley. "If you'd care to come into the castle now, I'll arrange an interview for you with Mr. Mariott." He climbed off his bicycle, started walking it back toward Blackwood Castle.

"Let's do that." Harry led his horse.

"There oughtn't to be any trouble about your visiting with him, Mr. Challenge," said the doctor. "Mr. Mariott, after all, isn't a prisoner."

Tubbs sneezed. Twice.

"Cease that grumbling," advised McMillion.

"I were sneezin', guv. Due, in good part, to bein' up to me bloomin' fundament in the dust of hantiquity."

"I do believe, old fellow, that I've unearthed something of considerable interest."

"Hunearthed is right. They oughter bury hall this musty—"

"Yes, this will come in deuced handy when we explore the castle."

The two of them were in one of the dim, dusty storerooms far below the Dunkelstein town hall.

"Was we hanticipatin' the exploration of some bloody old castle, guv?" Tubbs was at rest atop a knee-high stack of fat, ancient record books.

"We must have a look-see inside Blackwood Castle." The handsome journalist spread out the large architectural drawing he'd located in one of the venerable strongboxes. "This looks to be the original floor plan of the castle, showing— Hello, this is jolly interesting." He pointed to the margin.

"A plop of fly manure, is hit?"

"It happens to be an inscription, no doubt written in 1693 shortly after the castle was completed."

"Ham I safe in concludin' hit don't contain such news as'll cheer me up?"

"Apparently the architect, one Christian Steinbrunner, went stark raving mad just before the castle was completed."

"One of me cousins is married to a stonemason an'

there's a bloke could drive you bonkers if you was to work side by side with 'im for more 'n a—"

"What sent poor Steinbrunner round the bend is described as 'certain things that came up out of the unhallowed ground upon which the cursed castle is built.' Villagers found him late one rainy evening, running about in the woods and gibbering like a monkey. His hair had turned quite white."

"Can good times such as that still be hobtained in the vicinity? Sounds like hit'd put the bloomin' Crystal Palace ter shame."

McMillion was moving his gloved finger over the dusty plans. "Ah, yes. Yes, one could quite probably enter here . . . or even here, unobserved. Then we'd make our way through the crypt until—"

"Crypt? 'At's where they store the defunct members of the 'ouse'old, hain't it?"

"My, just look at this." He chuckled, moving his finger along a zigzag path. "A series of secret passages that will allow one to travel to all levels of the castle unseen."

Tubbs stood up and scratched at his groin. "Hain't it likely the doc knows hall them nooks an' crannies an' secret passways hin that pile?"

Rolling the drawing up carefully, McMillion then concealed it beneath his jacket. "Perhaps he does," he replied. "Yet that merely makes this even more challenging."

Chapter 17

"Couple of damn fools."

"They're quite concerned over you."

"Over my money, son."

Harry was sitting in an arbor at the south side of the castle grounds. Flowering vines climbed and twisted all up and over the white latticework surrounding him and the tea merchant.

The amiable Dr. Mistley had brought them together ten minutes ago, then discreetly withdrawn.

Glancing around the green lawns beyond the arbor, Harry said, "There's nobody around, Mariott. You can level with me."

"What the hell's that supposed to mean?" He was a thickset man of middle height. This morning he wore a lightweight cotton suit.

Harry had to admit to himself that the millionaire was looking healthier than he had in any of his recent photographs. "You're not being kept here against your will?"

"Where'd you get a tomfool idea like that, son?"

"Both your niece and nephew feel that—"

"My niece and nephew, you'll excuse my pointing out, Challenge, are a pair of ninnies. In fact, I strongly suspect Jack is—"

"Why did you refuse to see them when they were here?"

"I didn't wish to." He leaned forward in his wicker chair, rested a hand on his knee. "See here, son, I'll be honest with you. Boston is one of the most boring spots on the face of the earth. And those two mooncalves are about as dull as a bowl of cold porridge."

Several bees were buzzing around the blossoms of the arbor. Idly Harry watched them flickering through the warm air. "Just how long do you intend to remain here?"

"That's nobody's business but my own, son."

"Still Jack and Amy might feel better were you to set a specific . . ."

"A specific what, young man?"

"Date," said Harry casually, trying not to look directly at the bee who'd alighted on Mariott's thick neck. "If they knew exactly when you intended to come home they—"

"It's not beyond the realm of possibility, son, that I shall never return to Boston. When you consider how many wonderful romantic cities there are in the world, you— Just what are you gawking at, Challenge?"

Harry glanced away. "I was intent on catching your every word." The bee, Harry was damn sure, had stung the tea millionaire smack on the neck and then gone buzzing off. But Mariott hadn't even noticed.

That must be because he wasn't Mariott.

Nope, he was another of Dr. Mayerling's automatons. An even better one than any of those at the Pavilion of Automatons. Good enough to fool Harry, certainly.

Probably, though, they hadn't wanted to risk letting his close relatives get a look just yet. That's why Jack and Amy were turned away.

"Was there anything else, son?" asked the Mariott automaton impatiently.

Harry took out a cigar, cut off the end, lit it. "I do believe, sir, your kin would be relieved if you were to allow them to visit you and witness for themselves how well you're doing." He stood up.

"You ought to cease smoking," advised the automaton as he rose. "It can kill you."

"There are a hell of a lot of things on the list ahead of smoking," said Harry, taking another slow puff.

Dr. Mistley stopped beside a heavy wooden door in the cool stone corridor. "If you have a moment before departing, Mr. Challenge, I'd like very much to show you something," he said. "In my office."

"Sure, go ahead."

Smiling, the young doctor turned the brass knob and the door creaked open. "I trust your visit with Mr. Mariott was satisfactory."

"Certainly took a load off my mind."

The office was large, beam-ceilinged. The late morning light coming in through the three high narrow windows didn't quite rid it of its chill.

Crossing to a neatly kept desk, Mistley seated himself. "I understand you're a close personal friend of an excellent illusionist named the Great Lorenzo." His left hand rested on a glazed skull that served as a bookend.

"Yep, we're pals. Why?"

The young doctor picked up a small crystal sphere about the size of a baseball. "I suppose it's a foolish hobby for a man of science, yet I enjoy dabbling in parlor magic."

"A good place for it."

"Please don't let me bore you or take up too much of your valuable time." He hefted the crystal, which was cloudy now. "I did, however, very much want to show you this new trick I've just mastered."

"Proceed," invited Harry. Surely they weren't going to make another try at hypnotizing him?

The crystal grew cloudier. Smiling, Dr. Mistley threw it into the air. "Watch the crystal."

The globe remained floating, about four feet from the floor. Pulsing, glowing with a faint yellowish light, it drifted close to Harry.

"No strings?" he said.

"You ought to be seeing something about now."

Harry did.

Inside the crystal was an image of Jennie Barr. Her auburn hair was down and there was a dark bruise across her cheek. He saw only her head against a background of gray stone wall.

Slowly Harry got to his feet. "Where is she?"

The image left the crystal ball; the ball dropped to the rug.

"In a safe place," replied Dr. Mistley, smiling. "The moment you leave Orlandia, the young woman will be released." He stood to face Harry. "It won't be necessary, you see, to arrange for a meeting with Dr. Mayerling at all. You have forty-eight hours to consider. After that—"

"Nothing's going to happen to her."

"Oh, really?"

"Because if it does," Harry promised him, "something'll happen to you."

Chapter 18

Wearing a fluffy white chef's hat, white jacket and flowing white apron, the Great Lorenzo came hurrying along the Mariahilferstrasse just at dusk. He was carrying a small pig over his left shoulder.

From the Exposition grounds, merry waltz music wafted on the darkening air.

"I cut quite a figure on the dance floor in my youth," he confided to the pig. "Nimble was but one of the many glowing terms used to describe me. Adonis was— Ah, but we have arrived."

He stopped before the rear gate of the palace grounds. Through the wrought-iron bars he could see across the cobblestone yard to the brightly lit windows of the kitchens.

"Let's have some expediency," he boomed out. "I can't wait all the blessed night out here." He agitated the bellpull while kicking at the bars.

"Here, here, this is the palace." A uniformed guard came running up to the gate.

"I should hope so," said the magician, "since I'd feel foolish delivering this porker to the Kunsthistorisches Museum."

"We aren't expecting a pig."

"You aren't, the kitchen staff certainly is," the

Great Lorenzo informed him. "The royal physician, not an hour ago, telephoned Dinglehoofer's Grand Prix Butchery to order this very piglet." He lowered his voice. "It is hoped some pork chops will perk up His Majesty."

"They think so? Why, when I'm under the weather a greasy pork chop is the last item I'd—"

"Ah, but then you aren't a king," the magician reminded. "Now you'd best let me in, lest we both get in deep trouble."

The guard hesitated, gazing at the pig for several thoughtful seconds. "Very well. I don't want to interfere with His Majesty's health, poor fellow."

"Precisely, my boy." As soon as the gates swung a few feet open, the Great Lorenzo insinuated himself onto the palace grounds. "Now I must continue on my errand of mercy."

He trotted across the cobblestones while the twilight deepened all around.

Once inside the hallway connecting the kitchens, he stepped through the first open doorway.

A husky red-faced woman in white was standing by a wooden table, tossing salad in an immense copper bowl. "What?" she inquired, glowering at him.

"I've come with the pig."

"So I see."

Grunting, the Great Lorenzo placed the small pinkish creature down on the hardwood floor. "The interesting thing about this particular porker is—"

"Who are you? Why have you intruded into the royal kitchen?"

"The interesting thing about this pig," resumed the magician, "is that he isn't dead. Nay, merely hypnotized into a trancelike state. When I snap my fingers thusly— Voila! He awakens."

The little pig blinked, glanced around the huge room. Scrambling to his feet, he commenced to squeal loudly and run around the floor in anxious circles.

"Oh! Oh!" exclaimed the head cook. "That horrible thing. Ugh! Get him out of here." She began screaming, waving a wooden salad spoon in the air.

"I leave that chore to you, dear lady." Bowing out, he continued along the corridor.

Various other members of the culinary staff were emerging from various other doorways, curious.

"Terrible accident," the magician told one and all, pointing back. "Bloodshed, horror. Pigs running amok. Hurry."

They did and he raced off in the opposite direction.

"I do believe," the Great Lorenzo said to himself, "I've created a splendid diversion."

"Such trash," muttered the Great Lorenzo.

He was searching the ornate claw-footed bureau in the suite of rooms Baron Otto Van Horn had been occupying the past few weeks. The third stack of yellow-backed French novels in as many drawers had brought forth his critical comment.

"Does no one read of Deadwood Dick anymore?"

The magician was rummaging through Dark Otto's impressive collection of silk underwear, in search of something that would provide details on what had been done with the missing Wolfgang Spangler, when he heard approaching footfalls in the palace corridor outside.

Easing the drawer shut, he hurried to a closet. He crouched amid the highly polished riding boots, leaving the heavy door open a few inches.

Seconds later Dark Otto entered the suite, accompanied by someone else.

"Your performance this evening is faulty," the baron said, clicking on the electric lamp by his bedside. "One of the physicians went so far as to eye you curiously."

Some of the light came seeping into the closet, almost touching the hunkered magician.

"We've had far too much damp weather lately," replied the pleasant voice of Princess Alicia. "That always affects me, Otto."

"Yet that swine Spangler assured us you would not have such problems," complained Van Horn. "The king can't possibly live much more than a few days longer. When the old fool does expire, you must be able to assume the throne."

The princess had a very lovely laugh. "Don't fret so," she told the baron. "Was I not born to rule?"

Duchess Hofnung gave the Great Lorenzo an enthusiastic farewell hug. "My brave and courageous Renzo," she said, "you must promise to return safely to me."

"I fully intend to survive this venture, m'love."

They, with Helga Spangler close by, were on the platform at the Zevenburg rail station. The nine o'clock express to Dunkelstein was due to depart in six minutes.

"Do you really believe?" asked Helga, "that my father is a prisoner at Blackwood Castle?"

Nodding, the magician extricated himself from the grasp of the affectionate duchess. "So I learned, dear child, from my eavesdropping earlier in the evening."

"I still don't understand why they—"

" 'Twould take far more time than I can presently spare to explain this conspiracy to you now." Stooping, he gathered up his portmanteau and a long, thin package wrapped in butcher paper.

"Won't you at least tell us, Renzo, what's in that strange parcel?" asked the petite Duchess Hofnung, following him as he hurried toward his first-class compartment.

"A curio that I'm most anxious to deliver to Harry Challenge."

"Did you borrow it from the Lusitanian Pavilion at the Exposition, love? Is that the reason we had to stop there in our mad rush to—"

"Dear ladies." He opened the door of his compartment with a sweeping gesture. "Before many more days have passed into oblivion all will be made clear, crystal clear, to you." He carefully deposited his bag and his package inside.

From out of the night air he plucked two gardenias. He bestowed one on the duchess, one on Helga.

"Renzo, promise you won't try anything danger—"

"Farewell, adieu." After kissing his fingertips at both of them, the Great Lorenzo stepped into his compartment, shut the door and drew the shade.

Chapter 19

Harry kicked the door open.

"I thought so." He went striding into the room.

Seated at the small desk near the window was Peter Starr McMillion. He was wearing a silken smoking jacket with scarlet dragons embroidered on its back, and he had an architectural drawing spread out before him.

"Ah, hello there, Challenge. I was just thinking of going out for a spot of lunch," he said, smiling handsomely. "Care to join me for—"

"It's three in the afternoon."

"Is it really? Jove, how—"

"When I got back from Blackwood Castle yesterday, I had another talk with Professor Staub." Harry stopped in the center of the room. "He and—"

"I sent my man Tubbs out to invite you to dine with me last evening," said McMillion. "We might have, had you accepted my invitation rather than punching Tubbs in the face, compared notes." He gestured at the door to an adjoining room. "Poor chap's lying in yonder room with an icebag on his eye, cursing you and—"

"After Staub and I talked to Jennie's other contacts in town," Harry continued, "I came to the conclusion I'm going to have to sneak inside that damn castle, take care of Mayerling and then rescue Jennie."

The journalist chuckled. "Well, there, you see? You and I, old boy, have arrived at the same—"

"The problem is, and I didn't find this out until I'd spent six hours in the bowels of the town hall today, that you swiped the only existing copy of the—"

"So that's where you've been, eh, old boy? Wasn't going to comment on how dusty you look, but since you—"

"I want those plans." He crossed the room.

Pushing back in his chair, McMillion stood to face him. "Pause a moment, Challenge, and reflect," he suggested. "Granted you're a brave chap, capable of facing all sorts of hazards. Yet Dr. Mayerling is a formidable foe, ensconced in a fortress to boot."

"That I already know."

"Then accept my offer of assistance," said McMillion. "I've certainly proven myself a handy fellow in a tight spot. Surely you've read of my—"

"All your exploits are written up by you."

"Even so, I happen to be as honest and truthful as . . . as Henry Mayhew was in writing of the wretched poor of London. Why, I—"

"I don't need help."

"See here, Challenge, we all of us slip up now and then. Should you make a mistake now, it will jeopardize not only you but Jennie as well," he said. "I am correct in assuming that your primary motive in assaulting Blackwood Castle is to rescue Jennie Barr from therein?"

"She's in there, yes. I saw her yesterday."

"Saw her, did you? Jove, how is she faring under—"

"What I saw—" Harry glanced around, feeling a

sudden weariness. He walked to an armchair and sat. "Okay, McMillion, I'll accept your offer. But after I tell you what's really going on out there at the castle, you may not want to join in."

Throwing his shoulders back, McMillion assured him, "I've faced worse dangers than this and not flinched."

"I don't think so," said Harry.

Harry was in the courtyard of the inn that evening, smoking an after-dinner cigar, when the Great Lorenzo arrived. It was a clear, cool night and the sky was rich with stars.

Harry had been gazing upward, wondering what it might feel like to be three-hundred-some years old.

The carriage came rattling in under the archway. The magician and a tourist couple emerged. Both the man and the woman, middle-aged Italians, were carrying armfuls of roses and had puzzled expressions. The Great Lorenzo had obviously been entertaining them on the ride from the Dunkelstein station.

"Ah, Harry, my boy," exclaimed the magician when he caught sight of his friend. "You are the very object of my breathless pilgrimage." He handed him a long skinny package. "Carry this; I'll manage my portmanteau."

"Ow." Harry discovered he'd been given something with a blade. "What the hell is—"

"The Sacred Silver Sword of San Sebastian—try saying that some time with a lisp." He pushed on into the inn. "We must have a conference at once, lad."

"You planning to take rooms here?"

"I can bunk with you for the nonce."

"This way then." He led him upstairs to his room.

The magician gave the place a swift appraisal. "Better than a room in a Philadelphia hotel," he decided.

"How'd you come by the Sacred Silver Sword of San Sebastian?" He dropped the package on the foot of his bed.

"Swiped it from the Lusitanian display at the Exposition." Shedding his black cape, he draped it over a chair. "Had to hypnotize two guards plus several little pig-tailed lasses and their art teacher. A third guard proved a faulty subject. Him I conked with my cane."

"Aren't you supposed to be putting on a magic show just about now back in Zeven—"

"What is the basis for all true friendship? I'll tell you. Sacrifice. Greater love than this has no man and so on." The magician sighed, fluffed his side-whiskers. "At this very moment I fear my assistant and sometime understudy, a woefully inept illusionist named J. Randolph Cox is filling in for me. By now he's already botched the Devil's Buzzsaw illusion and is about to stumble through the Mandarin's Chest Myster— Ah, but no time to lament over the possible complete and total ruin of my show and my treasured reputation. Nay, I turned my back on all that to rush here to this tank town."

"Why exactly?"

"To lend a helping hand to you, why else?"

"Appreciate that," said Harry, sitting on the edge of the bed. "I could use some help, since I'm planning on leading a raid on Blackwood Castle in the hour just before dawn."

Nodding, the Great Lorenzo said, "Yes, and you don't know what I know."

"That's possible."

Settling into an armchair, the magician said, "I have learned much since we parted, Harry."

"Been having more visions?"

"No, not at all. I've been doing detective work. Yes, first-class crackerjack detective work, my boy." He held up a plump forefinger. "Firstly, Dr. Mayerling is no mere mortal. Ah, not at all. He is—and be prepared for a stunning surprise—he is a vampire."

"I know."

"You know?" A slightly crestfallen expression came over his face. "I risked life and limb, playing peeping tom within the walls of the Zevenburg Palace itself to learn this and you—"

"Friend of Jennie Barr's told me. See, Lorenzo, Jennie's been grabbed by Mayerling and—"

"That's exactly why I borrowed the silver sword, for use on the doctor. Nothing works better on a vampire than silver and— You and Miss Barr sound to be on a different footing than you were when you departed Zevenburg."

"That I'll fill you in on later. Do you have other reasons for rushing here?"

"I'd learned that Dr. Mayerling was considerably more dangerous than originally advertised. I naturally assumed you'd have need of a fellow who knew his way around in supernatural circles." He tapped his broad chest. "I have also uncovered facts you may not be in possession of, my boy. Do you know who Wolfgang Spangler is?"

Harry shook his head. "Nope. What's he got to do with—"

"Spangler is the key figure in the entire nefarious plot," answered the magician. "He is the premier builder and designer of automatons in all Europe.

Dr. Mayerling is in cahoots with none other than Baron Otto Van Horn, also known as Dark Otto. Dr. Mayerling lured Spangler from his hearth and home in Munich. They promised him a lucrative position with the Exposition in the Pavilion of Automatons, with which you are all too familiar. Instead they spirited the man away, putting him to work at fashioning insidiously clever mechanical reproductions of actual people."

"I met one of them yesterday."

The magician eyed him. "Who?"

"They've got an automaton version of old Mariott," answered Harry. "Damn convincing, too, and much better even than the gang in the pavilion."

Exhaling, the magician continued. "Spangler has been a prisoner of Blackwood Castle for several months," he said. "He has built, to my knowledge, at least one other nearly flawless simulacrum."

"Of whom?"

"The Princess Alicia," said the magician.

Chapter 20

"Jove, I knew my disguises would come in handy."

"Would yer move 'at bloomin' fiddle, guv, hit's diggin' inter me fundament."

"Don't thrash about so, Tubbs; you nearly brushed my moustache loose."

"Moustache, is hit? Looks more like a caterpiggle what—"

"Hush."

These voices were coming from within a canvas-covered wagon that was wending its way, with considerable creaking and rattling, along the predawn forest road.

At the reins, with a bold crimson bandanna on his head and a large golden ring dangling from his ear, was the Great Lorenzo.

Beside him, looking no different than usual, sat Harry.

"He isn't," remarked the magician, "a very convincing Gypsy."

"We aren't going to run into all that many people we'll have to convince," said Harry.

"Are you insinuating we don't even need this absolutely authentic Gypsy vehicle which I procured at considerable—"

"It's as good a way as any to get all of us to Blackwood Castle."

Up on some dark, unseen branch an owl hooted
mournfully.

"My boy, you're rather gloomy," remarked the
Great Lorenzo, his eyes on the swaying backs of
the two sturdy horses who were pulling the wagon
through the predawn woodlands. "Do you always
sulk on the eve of battle?"

"I feel easier when I work alone."

"In this instance you are going to need all the help
you can muster, Harry my lad. In fact, it might have
been a wise move to alert the local law so—"

"Sure, Lorenzo. We pop into police headquarters
and tell them we'd like some help going up against
Mayerling. Seems he's a vampire and—"

"We're not obliged to provide all the details of this
venture to—"

"And they better bring along plenty of artillery
because there are also probably going to be some mechanical men to overcome. Not to mention maybe a
stray werewolf or two plus—"

"Granted most coppers are not excessively imagina-
tive, yet they'd certainly understand kidnapping."

"We can't prove he's kidnapped a single soul."

"You saw the titian-tressed Jennie yourself when—"

"I saw her image in a crystal ball, Lorenzo. That's
not exactly admissible evidence."

"What about the Princess Alicia then? She, too, is
a prisoner of Blackwood Castle."

"All we have on that is your word."

Tugging at his earring, the magician asserted, "But
I heard Dark Otto discussing the whole vile plot while
I was lurking amid his excessively large collection of
boots. He, working closely with our own Dr. Mayerling,

forced Spangler to create a highly convincing mechanical replica of Princess Alicia. Once old King Ulrich kicks off, which sad event may occur any day now, they intend to put that clockwork imitation on the throne. The baron hasn't the nerve to seize power openly, but he yearns to become the gray eminence who—"

"Hearsay," put in Harry. "No law officer, here or in Zevenburg, would believe any of this."

" 'Tis true nonetheless."

"And that's why we're going to invade the castle. After we clean things up we can let the law know."

Shrugging, the Great Lorenzo said, "At least you ought to be encouraged about one thing."

"Which?"

"It wasn't the real princess who ordered them to give you the bum's rush at the palace," he replied. "Nor was she behind the attempts on your life. Dark Otto and Dr. Mayerling feared you'd spot a ringer if you got too close to their replica of your true love and thus they—"

"Alicia isn't exactly my true love."

"Ah? Do I detect a shift of your affections to some other quarter?"

Harry said, "We're nearly at Blackwood Castle. Start looking for a spot to ditch this wagon."

Tubbs hugged himself, whispering, "Gor, hit's colder nor a witch's jampot."

"I'd prefer, old man, that you suffer in silence."

The journalist and his valet were crouched on a wooded hillside a hundred yards from the rear of the castle wall. Ten minutes earlier Harry and the Great Lorenzo had gone downhill to try to gain entry by way of a hidden passageway in the stone wall.

"Whyn't we get the hinside arf of this bleedin' job,

guv? Hit's bound ter be warmer hinside that mauso-leum."

"In an operation of this sort, each man must play his assigned role." McMillion patted his flowing black moustache, then touched the handle of the re-volver tucked into his yellow sash. "Our job is to back up Challenge and the magician chap."

"I seen 'is show once, hin Bucharest. Punk stuff," commented Tubbs. "Honly interestin' thing ter look hat were a dark-'aired quiff wearin' a frock what barely succeeded hin coverin' 'er ladyjane an' then this stupid sod kept makin' 'er disappear."

"He seems a capable fellow, although a bit long-winded."

Hugging himself tighter, Tubbs inquired, " 'Ow long do we freeze our fundaments 'ere?"

The sun was rising now, a thin yellow light spread-ing through the trees.

"We're to wait an hour. Then we go in after them."

"Hif they hain't out in an hour, hit'll mean the gobblings got 'em," the shivering valet pointed out. "Hinstead of puttin' our own tails in the snare, guv, we ought to 'op in that wagon an' depart fer sunnier climes an' scenes."

"One doesn't desert one's comrades."

"Neither of them blokes his me comrades."

"Nevertheless."

"Hin fact, 'Andsome 'Arry the Boy Detective seems fair ter stealin' yer freckled grummett—yer lady reporter—from hunder yer bloomin' nose."

"We'll watch and wait in silence, old man."

Tubbs produced a grumbling sound.

The day grew gradually brighter, but the chill did not depart.

After a few moments Tubbs asked, "Hif yer hain't goin' ter win the wench, guv, what's hin this fer you?"

"A tremendous story," replied McMillion.

"We've done admirably thus far," observed the Great Lorenzo.

Harry nodded and held his oil lantern higher.

They were traveling along a narrow stone-walled passageway that snaked beneath Blackwood Castle. The gray stone blocks of the wall were rich with a thick, black, fuzzy mildew, and the damp air was fragrant with the smell of decay.

"Once in San Francisco, that fabled city beside the Golden Gate," said the magician as they moved along the passageway, "I briefly wooed a comely lady whose husband was a mortician by trade. Although she was striking in appearance, she always smelled just about like this tunnel. Thus, with some regret, I severed the—"

"Here's the wooden door."

"So it is." He consulted the notes he'd made after poring over the castle plans with Harry. "Yon portal ought to lead us right into the crypt."

"Which is where, according to Professor Staub, we find Mayerling snoozing in his coffin."

After rubbing his palms together, the magician took hold of the brass handle of the heavy wooden door. "Yes, vampires are noted for creeping back into their coffins once sunup arrives," he said, trying the handle. "And since rosy-fingered dawn was already touching the countryside when we effected our subtle entrance into this stronghold some moments ago, we'll surely find Dr. Mayerling safely tucked away and helpless.

"If the professor's right."

"He ought to be, my boy. Vampires are tradition-bound and almost always keep their coffins, spread with a layer of their native soil, in the handiest sepulcher."

"You've had considerable experience with vampires?"

"Some. I've led, as who should know better than you, a colorful— Ah, she's opening."

Amid some creaking and scraping, the door came open toward them.

Harry moved to the dark threshold, shining the lantern light into the musty stone room beyond. "Coffins," he reported.

"So I see."

The room was large and chill. On stone shelves around the shadowy walls rested ancient coffins. Sitting atop the lid of one was a disdainful, well-fed rat.

In the center of the room, with a path to them worn in the dust, rested two newer coffins. Black, gold-trimmed, they sat on low wooden platforms. Both coffins were open.

"Let's have a look." Harry entered the crypt, scattering the dust as he walked to the coffins.

Crouching, he looked down into the nearest of them.

"That is not the good doctor," said the magician as he knelt beside Harry.

"So she's one, too."

Asleep in the satin-lined box, arms folded over her breasts, was Naida Strand.

"Would this be Miss Strand?"

"Yep." Rising, Harry walked around to the other coffin. This one was empty. "He's not here, Lorenzo."

"That's odd. I thought all vampires went to sleep at dawn."

"Not all," said a voice in the shadows.

Chapter 21

From beneath his cloak the Great Lorenzo produced the Sacred Silver Sword of San Sebastian. "This ought to come in handy about now," he suggested as he passed the glittering blade to Harry.

Harry accepted it, setting the lantern down on the chill stone floor.

The figure across the room had stepped free of the shadows. It was Dr. Mayerling, judging from the descriptions Harry had collected. He was a tall, lean man, dark, with his black hair slicked down and parted exactly in the middle. He seemed no more than fifty.

"Ah, the dauntless Harry Challenge," Mayerling said. "I must say, you don't even live up to the dreadfully modest reputation you've earned as a keyhole peeper." He glanced briefly at the magician. "As for your frightfully fat friend . . ." Chuckling, he rolled his eyes.

Harry said, "If I understand my vampire lore correctly, this silver blade ought to take care of—"

"Don't be so horribly naive, Challenge. You surely don't believe I came to this little encounter totally unprepared." Shedding his own dark cloak, he revealed that he, too, possessed a sword. The lantern light made the filigreed hilt and the blade flash as he held it up. "In the course of a long and frightfully eventful life, I've had the opportunity to become rather an accomplished swordsman. Not that I'd have to be all that marvelous to dispatch a bumpkin such as you."

The Great Lorenzo made a negative sound.

Without warning Dr. Mayerling lunged at Harry with the blade.

Harry dodged, backstepped, brought up his own sword.

When Mayerling lunged again, employing as much of a *flèche* attack as the crypt allowed, Harry parried.

Their blades clacked and clanged against each other.

"I do think it only fair to inform you, dear boy," said Mayerling as their blades met again, "that I was laying out fellows a good deal more skilled than you in Berlin as far back as the late 1780s."

"Here's a lad with three whole centuries of dull anecdotes to dump on us," remarked the Great Lorenzo, who'd drifted off into the shadows somewhere.

Harry parried again, got in under the doctor's flashing blade and almost scored a touch.

The shadows of the two dueling figures were projected on the stone wall, long and distorted, by the lantern sitting on the floor.

All at once something came whizzing out of the darkness. It hit the doctor's head, hard, producing an unexpected bonging.

Mayerling's legs wobbled, buckled, then spread like a broken wishbone.

He fell over, hit the floor, lay still.

The Great Lorenzo stepped back into the light, re-

trieved the stone funeral urn he'd used on the doctor's skull. "I assumed you weren't especially com-
mitted to a fair fight."

"Not especially, no." Frowning some, he was gazing down at the sprawled doctor. "That pot made an
unusual noise when it connected."

"Rather a Chinese gong effect, wasn't it? Yes, I
noticed." He set the urn aside. "The doctor also
sounded rather like a gunnysack of plumbing sup-
plies falling off a wagon when he came to rest, too."

"Damn it, not another ringer." Down on one knee,
Harry tugged at the doctor's sleek black hair.

Three pulls and the hair and scalp came free, re-
vealing a metal skull beneath.

The magician observed, "Apparently Herr Doctor
Mayerling does abide by vampire tradition and sleep
days."

"But where?"

" 'Tis a large and roomy castle."

Harry rested his sword across the open coffin, the
one holding the dark Naida. He hefted up the urn,
used it as a hammer to ruin the automaton's head.
"Least we can incapacitate this decoy."

Shuddering once, the Great Lorenzo said, "I should
wallow in all this mixing of illusion and reality, yet
this little set-to has unsettled me some. I'd have
sworn this was the real article."

"If the Alicia automaton is this good, she'll make a
damn convincing queen." Harry stood.

"Ought we, do you think, render Miss Strand
harmless?" He coughed into his hand, rubbing his
foot across the stone floor.

"With the silver sword in her heart, you mean?"

"Merely a suggestion. We were planning to do as
much for Dr. Mayerling when we—"

"She won't awaken until nightfall," said Harry, picking up his sword. "We'll leave her here for now."

"Just as well," said the magician, sighing with relief. "Shall we seek Dr. Mayerling elsewhere?"

"If he's asleep, too, I'd rather concentrate on Jennie and the rest. We've used up too much time already just tangling with substitutes."

"Then I'll lead on to a secret passage that'll take us to an upper level of the castle."

"Let's go," said Harry.

They hadn't taken away Jennie's notebook. Perched on the window seat of her room high in the left wing of the castle, legs tucked under her, she was writing out an account of all that had befallen her since leaving Zevenburg. *Scribner's* ought to be interested, or maybe *McClure's* or *The Century.*

From her barred window she could see down across several miles of green forest. Two silky black carrion crows were circling in the morning air.

The handsome Harry Challenge . . .

"No, that's rather too trite," decided the reporter.

The manly, open-faced Harry Challenge . . .

"Now he sounds like a sandwich."

Speaking of Harry, where the heck was he? He must've realized by now that she was a prisoner here.

"Suppose he's already tried to storm this place and—"

She'd never been able to warn him about Dr. Mayerling's true nature. Harry might've barged in, not expecting to meet up with a vampire and—

"But he's smart. When I turned up missing, he'd have gone to Willie Staub."

Certainly, and the leonine professor would've—

Jennie flipped back over her last few pages, finding that, as she'd suddenly suspected, she'd used "leonine" twice to describe Professor Staub.

She chewed at the end of her pencil, gazing out the leaded windowpanes. The crows were swooping down toward the woodlands.

Maybe Harry had dismissed her from his mind. If he knew, as she now did, that the real Princess Alicia was also a prisoner here in Blackwood Castle, he might be concentrating solely on rescuing the princess.

"How can a man as bright and perceptive as Harry see anything in that insipid blond with—"

Not that Jennie had met the princess since becoming a fellow prisoner. All she knew about her was what she'd gathered from young Dr. Mistley when he dropped in now and then for a chat.

"Darn, I ought to be able to charm him into letting me go," she told herself. "Or at least into telling me if they've hurt Harry."

That was one of the things she hadn't been able to worm out of Dr. Mistley.

He was a bit strange, though, and maybe that was why she wasn't succeeding as much as she wanted. There was something a bit . . . unearthly about him. He wasn't a vampire, because she'd seen him more than once during the daylight hours. He wasn't a werewolf either. No, he'd sat right here in this room last evening, with a full moon out there in the misty night sky, and he hadn't even sprouted stubble.

Whatever Mistley was, though, he wasn't anywhere near as strange as Dr. Mayerling.

Mayerling had visited her only once. He'd given her gooseflesh. He was . . . decadent. Much like that young illustrator she'd interviewed in London last summer. The fellow who wouldn't openly deny the rumor that he slept with a skeleton most evenings.

The manly, good-natured Harry Challenge shared my journey from . . .

"Harry isn't exactly good-natured, either," she reminded herself, and crossed out the line.

A tapping came on the door.

"Yes?"

It had to be Dr. Mistley, who was so polite he knocked on the door even though it was locked and he had the key.

The key sounded in the lock, the door opened. Mistley came marching in, stiff-legged, smiling tensely.

Jennie hopped to the floor. "Bit early for a chat, isn't— Harry!"

Just behind the blond doctor came Harry. "Good to see you again," he said, grinning.

She noticed, as she hurried closer, he had his Colt .38 pointed at young Mistley's back. "Same here. I was fearful they might have killed you or worse."

"I've been attempting to assure Mr. Challenge," put in Dr. Mistley, "that you've been treated with the utmost consideration and—"

"Well, it's better than Devil's Island," she acknowledged, rubbing at the welt on her cheek.

"You were struck by mistake, believe me. The automaton had been specifically instructed to use a hypodermic syringe on you rather than—"

"Enough," mentioned Harry, shutting the door with his foot. "Any idea where Mayerling is, Jennie?"

"He sleeps by day."

"We haven't been able to determine where."

She indicated Mistley, jabbing her pencil in his direction. "He knows."

"Haven't been able to persuade him to confide, though."

"My loyalty to my employer, to say nothing of my physician's oath, makes it next to—"

"Tie him and gag him, can you, Jennie?"

She took down the gilded cords that held the drapes. "These ought to do the job," she said, setting about the task. "You alone?"

"Lorenzo's here, and your chum McMillion is backing us up outside."

"Oh, him? Whyever did you—"

"There was no need for any of this violence," cut in Dr. Mistley. "Knocking out the sanitarium staff, disabling our costly automatons. A calm and rational conversation could—"

Jennie thrust a pillowcase into his open mouth, tied it in place with another. "The princess is here, too," she said, frowning. "I feel obliged to inform you of the fact, in case you wish to desert me and rush off to—"

"Get to her next," said Harry, putting his gun back in his shoulder holster. "Lorenzo and I, using what he describes as impressive stealth and cunning, have pretty much crippled the crew here. People and mechanical men. There were seven of the former and three of the latter. Been a busy morning."

She guided Dr. Mistley over to the bed, tipped him over on top of it. "He's got keys to all the rooms."

"I have those now." Harry tapped his coat pocket and it jingled. "I kept him this long to make sure I found you."

"Well, you've found me, so now you can get to the princess. Don't let me keep—"

"Lorenzo's going to set Spangler loose."

"Yes, he's the one who's been making, against his will, all these lethal and highly believable mechanical people," she said. "Oh, and Mariott is two doors down from me. I can turn him free if you want.

"For a prisoner, you've been learning a lot."

"People, especially Dr. Mistley here, like to confide in me," she said. "I have a comfortable face."

"That you do." Harry came over and kissed her.

Chapter 22

McMillion consulted his watch, which he was keeping in a pocket of his colorful Gypsy vest. "Exactly an hour has passed by, old man," he announced.

"So hit 'as, an' what a gala, fun-filled hour hit's been." Tubbs was sitting with his back to the trunk of a mighty oak.

"One of us ought to venture forth into the castle, don't you know. Only sporting, since we promised to extricate Challenge should—"

"One! I 'ad the himpression we was contemplatin' a team effort, guv."

Readjusting his head scarf, the journalist said, "While reflecting on our original plan, I've come to the conclusion it would be far wiser for just one of us to enter Blackwood Castle at this juncture, Tubbs. Should anything be seriously wrong within, then I—that is, the chap remaining outside—could ride like the wind to Dunkelstein for succor."

"Yer can't heven ride like a gentle breeze on either of them bloomin' plow 'orses what come with the wagon."

"I'd do my best."

Nodding sourly, the valet got to his feet. "I feel hit's me bloomin' duty ter volunteer for this 'azardous mission, guv."

"Jolly. That's the spirit that has made the British Empire great."

" 'At's the same spirit what's caused many a bloke to get 'is diddlywhacker lopped off in some 'eathen land, too."

"Here's a lantern." McMillion hung it over Tubbs's elbow. "And here, old fellow, is that pistol I picked up in Dunkelstein. It fires silver bullets, as you may recall."

"Waste of money. Lead works just as—"

"Not on some of the creatures you may encounter inside the dark halls of Blackwood Castle." He pressed the weapon into Tubbs's hand. "To be on the safe side, use this on anyone you so much as suspect of being a vampire, a werewolf, witch, warlock—"

"Suppose I just pot hanythin' what moves. 'Ow'll that be?"

"Splendid. Spoken like a true warrior."

"I'll be gettin' on with it then." Saluting with the hand that held the gun, Tubbs turned and began making his way down through the morning forest.

"Permit me to introduce myself," said the Great Lorenzo, stepping into the long, beam-ceilinged workshop. "I am none other than the Great—"

"Who are you?" A broad-shouldered man of fifty-five, wearing a leather cobbler's apron over his clothes, jumped up from behind the cluttered workbench at the center of the room.

"I happen to be, since you apparently don't recognize my world-renowned face, the Great—"

"How'd you get in here? Only Dr. Mayerling and—"

"A lock like this is mere child's play for—"

"I'm doing the best I can trying to finish this job. Interrupting me like this isn't going—"

"Sir, I've come to rescue you."

The other man set down the soldering iron he'd been using. Stretched out upon the table was the metal skeleton of a man-size automaton. Propped against a jug at the side was what looked to be the head of a prosperous middle-aged gentleman.

"Rescue me? I don't—"

"You are Wolfgang Spangler, are you not?"

"Yes, of course. Do I know you?"

"All the world knows the Great Lorenzo." He strolled over to the worktable to pick up the wax head and scrutinize it. "This is Sir Robert Briney, is it not?"

"Yes, and such trouble I've had with the speech mechanism you wouldn't believe," sighed Spangler. "Sir Robert is forever saying, 'Harumph, harumph . . . Gad, sir. Harumph . . . I meant to say . . . Harumph.' " He shook his head. "Try building that into a clockwork speaking device."

Setting the head aside, the magician surveyed the room.

Two other mechanical men, complete save for their heads, rested in armchairs against the far wall. There were bits of wire, scraps of metal and glass scattered all across the hardwood flooring.

"By the way," said the Great Lorenzo, "I bring you greetings from your daughter Helga."

"Helga. She is well?"

"Doing splendidly, sir, for a lass who's been pining away for her missing father."

"They wouldn't allow me to write or—"

"All such tribulations are in the past." He gestured toward the open doorway. "We can depart."

"I won't even have to finish Sir Robert?"

"That," the magician told him, "is but one of the many blessings of freedom."

She was standing by a large stained-glass window, and the morning sun tinted her long golden hair a delicate pink. Her gown was a floor-length one of white satin, high-waisted and simple in design.

She recognized him at once.

"Harry," she said, smiling a bit sadly, "are you a prisoner of this awful man, too?"

"Nope." Pocketing the borrowed keys, he came into her tower room. "Nobody's a prisoner anymore."

She frowned briefly before moving gracefully to him. "You mean you've rescued me?"

Harry nodded. "Along with the others."

Princess Alicia laughed gently and stepped close to put her arms around him. "I should have known, Harry," she said, pressing her lovely cheek against his chest, "that no matter where you were in the world, as soon as you heard I was in trouble, you'd come to save me."

Very carefully he put his hands on her slim shoulders and pushed her to arm's length from him. She was as pretty as ever. "That's not exactly how it was, Alicia."

Her bright blue eyes opened wider. "Then you didn't fight your way into Blackwood Castle for me?"

"You were part of it, certainly. Thing is, I don't

want you getting the notion—" Shrugging, he let go of her and turned away.

None of this was what he'd planned to do or say when he finally reached the princess.

Behind him she asked, "What of my father?"

"He's still alive."

"Yet no better?"

"No."

"You'll take me back to Zevenburg?"

He faced her. "Sure, soon as we clear things up here."

"I must be in the palace during—"

"There's going to be a problem at the palace," he told her. "How much do you know about why Mayerling's been holding you here?"

"Nothing. He's only spoken to me twice since I was kidnapped and brought here."

"There's another Alicia in the palace."

"How can that be?" She pressed one hand to her breast. "A girl who looks something like me?"

"A dead ringer, Alicia."

"But how—"

"She's an automaton, a mechanical replica who—"

"No one would be taken in by such a creature."

"Right now, with an assist from Dark Otto, she's fooling just about the whole damn country."

"Otto," said the princess. "Yes, I see. He's behind this."

"He and Dr. Mayerling. The idea is to put this fake on the throne after your father dies. The power behind the throne'll be Baron Otto Van Horn."

"And they kept me alive in case anything went wrong," she said. "Once this . . . replica is crowned, they'd have no need for me."

"None of that'll happen now."

She said, "I shall have a fight on my hands when I return to the capital."

"A hell of a fight, yes."

"You'll help me?"

Harry put a hand in his trouser pocket. "Sure, because I don't consider this business is finished until all the loose ends are tied up."

"Good, then I am confident all will go well," she said, smiling at him. "And, Harry . . ."

"Yes?"

She touched his arm. "What happened between us a year and more ago," she said quietly. "That really is over and done, isn't it?"

"It is," he answered, just now realizing that it was.

Chapter 23

Sir Robert Briney was saying, "Gad, sir . . . Harumph, harumph . . . What's the meaning of all this, what?"

Spangler nudged the Great Lorenzo. "See what I mean?"

They were gathered in the tapestried great hall of the castle, all the freed patients and other prisoners as well as the captive members of the sanitarium staff.

"Son, I suggest we make immediate plans to vacate," Jonah Mariott told the magician.

"Just as soon as Harry Challenge returns with the fair Princess Alicia we shall—"

"Malarkey." Jennie, notebook in hand, had been interviewing as many people as she could. "Harry and that blond are probably smooching up in the tower and won't be down here for hours yet."

"Ah, the proverbial green-eyed monster rears its—"

"Gad, now what, eh? Harumph, harumph . . . Are we to be invaded, I mean to say, by Gypsies and fuzzywuzzys, what?"

Peter Starr McMillion had just entered, somewhat cautiously, through the wide open front door. "Hello

155

there, Jennie." Smiling handsomely, he came striding toward her with hand outstretched. "This is a
jolly reunion, isn't it? It certainly appears, yes, as
though our rescue efforts have been most fruitful."

"Your moustache is drooping," the reporter informed him. "Better patch it up."

"It's supposed to droop, don't you know. Yes,
Gypsy moustaches are notoriously droopy." He was
glancing around the vast hall. "I say, you haven't
chanced to see my man, have you?"

"The loathsome Tubbs? Nope."

"Strange, since I dispatched the fellow into this
place quite a— Mr. Lorenzo, sir, have you noticed
Tubbs about?"

"No, I . . ." The magician hesitated, then pressed
his side.

Jennie hurried over to him. "Are you ill?"

He shook his head. "No, child, merely suffering
from an uninvited vision." He snapped his pudgy fingers at McMillion. "Come along with me, my boy,
and we'll retrieve the loyal Tubbs. Jennie, tell Harry
we'll return shortly."

"Where are we off to?" inquired McMillion.

"Below," replied the Great Lorenzo.

The magician moved once more along the rear
wall of Dr. Mayerling's deserted office. "Ought to be
just about here," he murmured. "Trouble with these
visions of mine is they don't always come in perfect
crystal-clear focus."

"What precisely are we seeking?"

"A slight navelesque depression is what I saw in—
Aha, this must be it." He pushed against a spot on
the stone wall.

A low rumbling commenced. The stone wall shiv-

ered, the doctor's collection of framed diplomas rattled. Then a door-size section of wall swung open.

"I say, there was no mention of this on the plans."

"We overlooked the obvious fact that the good doctor must have made more recent additions to his
store of hidden passages and secret rooms."

"And your vision tells you that Tubbs is to be
found beyond there somewhere?"

The Great Lorenzo picked up the lantern he'd set
on the doctor's heavy wooden desk. "Let us see." He
ventured into the corridor on the other side of the secret door. "Very little dust underfoot, indicating fre-
quent and recent use."

"One notices a rather unpleasant odor." McMillion, carefully, followed him.

"That'd be Dr. Mayerling."

"The blackguard is down here, is he?"

"He was." The passageway was taking them down
and down.

"I find your conversation a bit cryptic at times, old
man."

The magician trotted down a short flight of stone
steps to stop before a wooden door. "Hold this." He
passed the lantern back to his companion.

Crouching, he fished a lockpick from an inner
pocket and set to work. The task took little more
than three minutes.

Hand on the knob, he called out, "It's us, my dear
Tubbs." Then he opened the door.

Tubbs, the silver bullet pistol on his lap, was
slouched in an armchair. "Gor, 'ad I but known 'e'd
reek so, I'd never of shot the beggar."

The room they entered was much like a bedchamber, except instead of a bed there was a coffin at its
center.

Jerking the kerchief off his head and pressing it over his nose and mouth, McMillion approached the open coffin. "Jove, what a sight. A putrefying corpse I once encountered in Calcutta looked hale and hearty by comparison to this."

"The late Dr. Mayerling, if rumor is to be credited, lived a long full life," said the Great Lorenzo, glancing into the coffin. "But three hundred years of hard living has a way of catching up with you. Used silver bullets on him, did you, Tubbs?"

"That was hall I 'ad, guv." He stood, gesturing vaguely with the gun. "I stumbled in 'ere by purest haccident. I was explorin' hup habove an' paused ter strike a bloomin' match an'—well, I muster brushed hagainst a brass dingus on the wall. Next thing I knows, I'm fallin' through the floor and landin' on me fundament right smack next to this casket."

The Great Lorenzo squinted up at the ceiling. "And then the trapdoor shut fast after you."

"Right yer are, guv. Trappin' me in this 'ole," said Tubbs. "Well, yer may not credit this next, but this bloke sits right hup in his casket and glares hat me somethin' fierce." He shrugged. "I shot 'im."

"Good work, old man." McMillion clapped him on the back. "You've rid the world of a prime scoundrel."

"I weren't hexpectin' 'e'd smell so foul afterwards. An' me stuck 'ere for all heternity maybe."

"We can leave now." The Great Lorenzo shut the lid of the coffin.

Chapter 24

The Great Lorenzo hummed as he walked. "This reminds me of a parade I once led through the thoroughfares of Youngstown, Ohio," he said. "Although we don't have Rollo the Ferocious Wild Man of Sulu along this time."

"And we're bringing up the rear of this one and not leading," added Harry.

He and the magician were at the tail end of a procession consisting of their Gypsy wagon, two borrowed farm carts and whatever released patients couldn't fit in the horse-drawn vehicles. Tubbs was driving the wagon.

"Although we've overcome Dr. Mayerling," said the magician as they made their way through the afternoon forest, "we still can't consider ourselves safe in port."

"Not with that spurious Alicia still extant, no." Harry had both his hands in his trouser pockets.

"We must work out a strategy to cope with the situation."

Harry said, "Hell, we'll just walk into the palace and confront Dark Otto and his automaton."

"Force, as well as cunning, may be needed to gain entry."

"We've got the real Princess Alicia; that ought to get us through the damn gates."

Bending, the Great Lorenzo picked a fallen oak leaf from the roadway. "Speaking of the true and authentic princess, my boy," he said while crumbling the leaf in his palms, "do I detect a certain coolness twixt you twain?"

"Probably so."

"Alas." He opened his hands and a yellow finch flew out and away. "I've been considering yours one of the great romances of the decade."

"Dime novel stuff," said Harry.

After humming to himself for a few moments, the magician said, "Still and all, Harry, if you hadn't tried to pay that call on the princess and gotten thrown out on your ear, why, this whole conspiracy might well have succeeded. A great many people would've been hurt."

"Remind me," said Harry, "to ask Princess Alicia to give me a medal."

The rain began while they were still a half mile outside of Dunkelstein. It was a slow chill rain that made the dust of the road smoke.

They heard the bells then, too, tolling mournfully from the town's three churches and the town hall tower as well.

"I fear," said the Great Lorenzo, "this means bad news."

"Yep, the king must've died," said Harry, "and word's reached here."

"We can't get back to Zevenburg until tomorrow night. By then Dark Otto's clockwork princess will be queen of the whole country."

"Maybe not." Harry ran through the rain to the Gypsy wagon.

He hopped up on the back step, let himself in through the rear door.

The princess was riding inside, sharing the wagon with Jennie and three of the female patients.

Jennie had her open notebook on her lap. "What's wrong, Harry?"

"The bells," he said.

The golden-haired princess was sitting on a folded blanket. "My father is dead," she said quietly. "That is why the bells are ringing."

"This changes things some," Harry told her. "When we get back to Zevenburg this ringer'll be queen."

Jennie said, "They have to crown her first."

"Hey, that's right," remembered Harry. "And they won't hold the coronation until after the funeral. So maybe we have enough time to—"

"There is some precedent," said Alicia with a sad shake of her head, "for having the coronation while the last monarch lies in state. Not every new ruler has done that, but Dark Otto certainly will."

"How soon could they crown the automaton."

"As soon as tomorrow perhaps."

Harry said, "Here in Dunkelstein they probably don't know Princess Alicia is supposed to be residing in the capital at this very moment. We're going to the train station, Alicia, and you're going to order us a special express train."

"Yes, but that may only gain us a few hours, Harry."

"A few hours may be enough," he said.

The head conductor found Harry in the smoking

car of the special express that was speeding through
the rainy night toward Zevenburg. "You are certain,
Herr Challenge, that Her Highness is satisfied with
the accommodations?"

"Everything's fine," Harry assured him. He'd
been sitting alone, smoking one of his thin cigars.

Taking off his gold-braided hat, the small plump
conductor wiped his forehead. "We usually have on
the line a much more luxurious car than the one the
princess is traveling in," he explained. "Unfortunately, some rowdies derailed it a few nights ago and
it lies, badly damaged, at the bottom of the Wohn-
zimmer Ravine. When we pass I'll point it out to you,
although in the rain and dark you probably—"

"No need." Harry exhaled smoke. "Although I
should think you'd be more careful about whom you
allow to use that private car."

"Oh, the gentleman who rented our splendid car is
not the one who shoved it off the tracks, no. He is, so I
am given to understand, an author of faultless reputation. Englishman." The conductor returned his hat
to his head. "It was, we believe, Gypsies who caused
the accident. Or possibly anarchists."

"Or both."

"That well may be." He bowed. "If there is anything further the railroad can do, Herr Challenge,
you have but to—"

"Thanks."

When the conductor was gone, Harry stretched up
out of his chair and stepped out on the observation
platform. Night was closing in, rain was hitting hard
on the metal awning that protected the observation
area.

Harry took a final puff of his cigar before flinging
it out into the wet darkness.

"It's only me," announced Jennie, stepping out to join him.

"So I noticed."

"Didn't want you to think I was a lycanthrope or an automaton."

"Very few freckled werewolves in the world."

She shrugged. "I've never seen any figures on the matter." Jennie was wearing the jacket of her travel suit over her shoulders and she adjusted it now, shivering once as she glanced out at the rain. "You've been, I can't help noticing, very glum since we left the castle."

"You know how it is when a vacation's over."

She sat on one of the two metal chairs. "Oops, this is damp."

"Not surprising."

"Off the record, Harry. Did you and the princess have a falling out?"

"Nope."

"Then your romance is still on?"

He shook his head. "No."

She pulled her jacket tighter around her. "Of course, we still have quite a few hurdles to overcome when we reach Zevenburg tomorrow afternoon. Just about everyone believes that insipid automaton is the real thing," she said. "So if we don't play our cards just right, we could be executed for treason or thrown in prison. Dark Otto isn't an admirable person. Well, he couldn't be and have a nickname like that, could he? And if you're brooding about what the outcome of everything is going to be, why, I guess that's a good enough reason for your being glum and sour-faced, and it hasn't a thing to do with whether the princess and you . . . whether the queen and you are in love or not."

Harry laughed. He sat down in the other chair. "When I got into this damn mess it was because I thought I was in love with the princess," he said. "There were all sorts of handicaps and odds against it and barricades. I'd worried about all that, which was one of the reasons I stayed away from Orlandia for a year or more. When I came back, though, I figured maybe I'd be able to work something out in spite of all the difficulties."

"Now you believe you can't?"

"Now I believe, Jennie, that I'm not in love with Alicia."

"Well, that's surely a good reason for being down in the mouth. You have an ideal, a goal and then it all . . ." She gestured at the rainy night. ". . . fades away on the wind."

"I'm gloomy, if I am gloomy, because I think I'm hooked on somebody else," he said. "And this girl is an even worse bet. She's as independent and feisty as I am. She roams the world like I do, a real loner most of the time, and she's not at all demure and ladylike. She's a damn good investigator, and a fair shot. We more than likely wouldn't get on together at all. She has freckles."

After a silence of several seconds, Jennie stood up. "Oh," she said quietly, and went away.

Chapter 25

Duchess Hofnung came hurrying along the afternoon train platform. "My darling Renzo," she cried, arms outspread. "I rushed here as soon as I received your wire." She hugged him. "I am so glad you survived."

"I share your sentiments, m'love," he said. "But what of the coronation?"

"It is going on even as we speak, dear. I don't quite understand why—my heavens!" She'd caught sight of the true princess alighting from the express on Harry's arm. "Oughtn't she to be at St. Norbert's Cathedral?"

"She ought, yes," agreed the magician. "We'll borrow your estimable carriage and deliver her."

"Haven't you time, Renzo, for a small snack and a bottle of—"

"Duty calls, my pet."

Harry and the princess joined them. "Is it on?" he asked.

"Right now." The Great Lorenzo paused, took in the gratifying scene of Helga Spangler reunited with her father, then started trotting toward an exit. "The dear duchess has kindly offered us her swift carriage."

"Let's go then."

All along the platform the rescued patients of the Blackwood Castle sanitarium were disembarking from the special train. Some still wore looks of bewilderment.

"What about the ladies and gentlemen of the press?" asked the Great Lorenzo as he spotted the duchess's carriage at the curb.

"Let them get their own transportation," said Harry.

"Are you and the charming Miss Barr no longer chums, my boy?"

Harry helped Princess Alicia into the carriage. "I think maybe I frightened her last night," he told the magician.

"We'll discuss the matter at some length after we put the royal house in order." He climbed up beside the uniformed driver. "To the coronation, my lad."

Harry had to fight one more duel.

Their carriage couldn't get closer than two blocks to the cathedral, then the crowds were too thick to move through. Abandoning it, Harry, Princess Alicia and the Great Lorenzo started along the Singerstrasse on foot.

"Make way, make way," ordered the magician in a booming voice. "Can't have a coronation without a princess."

"Mother of mercy! It's Princess Alicia!"

"Can't be. She just went into the cathedral."

"Don't I know the princess when I see her, dumbhead?"

"Who's a dumbhead?"

"The princess!"

"It's she! It's Princess Alicia!"

"Three cheers for the queen!"

"Long live the queen!"

On the wide marble steps of the towering Gothic-style cathedral three uniformed guards stepped forward to keep them out.

"No one is allowed in— Oops." The guard blinked. "Forgive me, Your Highness."

"Um . . ." said another of the guards timidly. "Didn't you already enter once, Your Royal Highness?"

"She did indeed," explained the Great Lorenzo, "yet she was so impressed by the showing you lads made, she had to slip out for another look. She's quite pleased with you all. Now, step aside so—"

"Yes, to be sure." All three clicked their booted heels and saluted.

The interior of the lofty cathedral was packed with people—dignitaries, officials, royalty. Altar boys in scarlet cassocks and crisp white surplices, dozens of yellow-haired, bright-faced tykes, lined the wide center aisle. The scent of sharp incense and hundreds of burning candles was thick in the air. A huge unseen organ was roaring out a majestic hymn.

Up on the scarlet-carpeted altar, amid the myriad candles and gilded candelabras, stood the Bishop of Zevenburg himself, a doddering gentleman of ninety-one, weighted down by the gold and crimson robes and miter. He held a bejeweled gold crown in his quivering old hands.

Kneeling before him was the Alicia automaton, lovely in a flowing gown of white silk.

Baron Otto Van Horn, in a uniform of crimson, gold and silver, stood stiffly nearby.

". . . in the eyes of God and in the eyes of man," the bishop was intoning in his thin reedy voice, "you,

beloved and divinely chosen Princess . . . Princess
. . . um . . . what is her dratted name?"

"Alicia," whispered one of the brightly robed
priests who shared the wide altar area with him.

"Eh?"

"Princess Alicia!"

"Of course, of course . . . um . . . where was I?"

" 'Beloved and divinely chosen . . .' "

"To be sure, to be sure . . . Ahum . . . Beloved and
divinely— Eh? What's this? A commotion in the very
main aisle of the St. Norbert's Cathedral?" The old
bishop gasped, staring at the determined approach of
the trio.

"Before you continue," said Harry, "you'd better
take notice that this is the true princess."

"Get this crazed swine out of here!" ordered Dark
Otto, glaring. "The man's a known assassin who—"

"Wait, wait," said the perplexed bishop as he
squinted beyond the automaton at the real princess.
"This seems most unusual. In all my years of officiat-
ing at such sacred ceremonies, never have I had *two*
candidates for—"

"Seize them!" The baron, face flushed with anger,
was waving and pointing.

The Great Lorenzo stepped casually up beside
the still-kneeling automaton replica of the princess.
"Your Excellency," he said to the bishop, "please
watch my hands closely."

Swiftly and unexpectedly, the magician snatched
at the mechanical woman's golden locks. The wig
came off and he flung it aside.

"Behold. A metal dome beneath." The Great Lorenzo knocked on the naked skull, producing a metallic bong.

"You idiot!" said the bald automaton, rising and backing away from him.

"It's your fault, Challenge," accused Dark Otto. "You intruded into my affairs! Ruined months of hard work and cunning preparation. You . . . you swine!" From the gilded scabbard at his side he jerked out a wicked sword. "Even though my scheme has vanished like the wind, yet I mean to have satisfaction. I'll gut you like the pig you are!"

"Fellow's obsessed with porkers." The Great Lorenzo reached under his dark cloak. "You'll need this trinket again, Harry my boy." He produced the Sacred Silver Sword of San Sebastian and tossed it down to his friend.

Harry caught it, grinned and nodded at Dark Otto. "You were saying?"

"Swine!" The baron charged down the carpeted altar steps at Harry.

"Stop," gasped the shivering bishop. "You cannot fight in this sacred place." He scowled at the magician. "And you, sir, what are you doing with a priceless relic that has recently been reported stolen?"

Harry and the baron faced each other on the scarlet-carpeted center aisle of the great cathedral.

Most of those who'd come to witness the coronation were on their feet now, talking, shouting, muttering. The organ continued to play from the loft far above.

Dark Otto lunged.

Harry parried.

"Five pfennigs the American wins," said one of the cherubic altar boys to the next one in line.

"Taken. Dark Otto'll finish him in a trice."

The baron had an aggressive style, greatly favoring a running attack. He was very angry now, though, taking risks.

Harry, patiently and calmly, parried his every thrust.

The organ, wheezing enormously, ceased playing. The spectators fell silent. The clash of the sword blades echoed through the vaulted cathedral.

Dark Otto made a misstep, was off balance for an instant.

Harry slipped in under his guard, his blade cutting into the baron's side.

Staggering, cursing, Dark Otto stumbled back.

Harry struck again, slashing the weapon out of his opponent's grip.

The baron's sword spun through the air, landed at the bishop's feet.

Glaring at Harry, Dark Otto spread his arms wide. "Go ahead, swine. Finish me off."

Harry eyed him for several long silent seconds. Then he grinned. "Hell, you're not worth the trouble."

He handed his sword to the Great Lorenzo. Turning on his heel, Harry went striding out of the cathedral.

Chapter 26

The Great Lorenzo was sitting opposite Harry in the train compartment, gazing out at the activity on the twilight platform. "You're making a rather abrupt departure, my boy," he remarked. "A mere three days after the fair Alicia is crowned queen, you hop on a crack train heading out of the country. Think of the various benefits that might shower on a brave and courageous chap such as yourself. Why, you're something of a national hero, and that, if exploited just right, should be worth several thousand—"

"You're the real hero of the piece," Harry told him, lighting his cigar. "Getting us to the church on time, providing me with a weapon to use against Dark Otto."

"True," admitted the magician modestly. "And you ought to see how my new notoriety is beefing up the box office. I am seriously thinking of extending my engagement another month and adding several more matinees per week."

"Well, I wasn't in the mood to linger in Zevenburg anyway," said Harry. He took a cablegram out of his coat pocket and passed it to the magician. "On top of which—"

"Ah, I sense the kindly hand of your warm-hearted old dad."

Dear son: You've cleaned up that mess, so quit sitting around on your duff. Get to Paris quick. We've got a new client who thinks maybe his Egyptian mummy has been taking walks of an evening. Sounds like moonshine, but he's got a stewpot of money to spend. Your loving father, the Challenge International Detective Agency.

Refolding the cable, the Great Lorenzo returned it to Harry. "Did you and Queen Alicia part friends?"

"We'll always be pals."

"Looks like Dark Otto will be exiled rather than made to languish in a dank cell."

"That's one of the advantages of being royalty."

The magician said, "Did you chance to see a copy of today's edition of the European version of the London *Graphic?*"

"Isn't it there among the stuff you materialized for my trip?"

After searching through the scatter of fruit baskets, flowers, newspapers and magazines on the seat beside him, the Great Lorenzo shook his head. "Seems I neglected to provide one. At any rate, our recent comrade-in-arms, Peter Starr McMillion, penned a true account of the Dark Otto–Dr. Mayerling affair for the sheet. You may be surprised to learn that it was Pete and not we who masterminded the raid on Blackwood Castle as well as the showdown at the cathedral. He does, almost as a footnote to his stirring autobiographical account, mention he had some small bit of help from 'a little-known

American private inquiry agent and a music hall entertainer.' Music hall!"

"Doesn't sound like anything you'll want to paste in your scrapbook."

"They even ran a drawing of him in that Gypsy outfit." Sighing, the magician rose to his feet. "Have a pleasant journey, my boy. I must return to the theater and prepare to astound my early show audience."

Harry held out his hand. "Thanks, Lorenzo."

Shaking hands, the Great Lorenzo said, "We'll meet again. I'm certain we will, since I had a vision about it only this morning. Won't give you any details now, so as not to spoil the surprise of it. Adieu."

He stepped out onto the platform and went walking away into the twilight.

The train crossed the border at a few minutes before midnight.

Harry was sitting in his compartment, reading at one of the novels the Great Lorenzo had given him. The story had to do with a murder and other foul deeds at a vast, gloomy English countryhouse. The detective on the case wasn't particularly bright.

Someone tapped on his door.

Shutting the novel without bothering to insert a bookmark, Harry said, "Yes?"

The door opened and Jennie Barr's freckled face looked in. "I heard there was an American detective on board," she said, "so I decided to take a peek. See if it was anyone I knew."

"C'mon in," he invited.

"Somewhat late."

"Even so."

She entered, closed the door carefully behind her and sat facing him. "You're leaving Orlandia?"

"Seem to be. You?"

Jennie smiled. "My editor was so pleased with the stories I wired him, he told me to take two weeks off. With pay."

"And you're going where?"

"Paris. I always like Paris, especially in the spring," she replied. "Where are you traveling to?"

"Paris. A new case."

"Isn't that an amazing coincid— Well, actually it isn't, Harry."

"Lorenzo told you I was taking this train and where I was bound for."

"Matter of fact, he did."

Nodding, Harry said, "He didn't mention you at all during our farewell chat. I figured that was the reason."

She reached into her shoulder bag. "He present-ed me with this," she said, extracting a bottle of brandy. "From Duchess Hofnung's own cellar, al-though she may not know it."

"There are a couple of glasses in that picnic ham-per, next to the hard-boiled eggs," said Harry.

"You open this then." She handed him the bottle. "I'll find the—yes, here they are."

"Okay, the bottle's opened."

Jennie smiled and moved across the compartment to sit beside him.

BIO OF A SPACE TYRANT
Piers Anthony

"Brilliant...a thoroughly original thinker and storyteller with a unique ability to posit really *alien* alien life, humanize it, and make it come out alive on the page."

The Los Angeles Times

Widely celebrated science fiction novelist Piers Anthony has written a colossal new five volume space thriller—**BIO OF A SPACE TYRANT:** *The Epic Adventures and Galactic Conquests of Hope Hubris.*

VOLUME I: REFUGEE   84194-0/$2.95
Hubris and his family embark upon an ill-fated voyage through space, searching for sanctuary, after pirates blast them from their home on Callisto.

VOLUME II: MERCENARY   87221-8/$2.95
Hubris joins the Navy of Jupiter and commands a squadron loyal to the death and sworn to war against the pirate warlords of the Jupiter Ecliptic.

VOLUME III — Coming Soon

ALSO BY PIERS ANTHONY: